A Voice in
the Darkness

Margaret James

A Voice in the Darkness

St. Martin's Press
New York

Library of Congress Catalog Card Number: 78-21423

ISBN 0-312-85079-4

ONE

On the 18th September 1870, Eliza Dodds disappeared.

At six o'clock she left the house of Miss Lucy Morton, the village dressmaker, and was seen a few minutes later by the stable-boy who worked at *The Sexton's Arms*. At ten minutes past the hour she was observed by Mrs. Trout, housekeeper to Dr. Sawyer of the Old Mill, trotting up Colley's Walk towards the church, lying on the northern edge of Easton Mallet. After that, she was never seen again.

Later, Mrs. Trout was voluble in her insistence that the fourteen-year-old maid-of-all-work had been in good spirits. She was smiling, said Mrs. Trout loudly to those who had gathered about her; swinging a basket on her arm, neat and trim in a dark print dress covered by a clean white apron.

When it became obvious that Eliza had not reached her destination, the grey stone cottage where her cousin, Kate Plum, cared for her orphaned brothers and sisters, some kind of search was made for the missing girl. Kate's distress was real enough to move a few of the neighbouring farmhands to comb the nearby woods, and one or two of them even went as far as Calder Bottom, well outside the village, but to no avail.

Tongues wagged for a full two days. Some whispered that Eliza had run away from Lucy Morton's service, for although the dressmaker had no money to speak of, her standards were high, and she had kept Eliza on the run from morning to night. Then others recalled that only three months before, another girl had vanished. Ada Mullins, aged fifteen, also in the service of Miss Morton. It was odd, right enough. The village women, gathering in Mr. Tyght's grocery store, ekeing out their pennies on an ounce or two of tea and a few currants for a boiled pudding, shook their heads.

But the speculations and gossip did not last for long, for really they all knew what had happened to Eliza, and to Ada Mullins too, for that matter. Lucy Morton might have been a hard mistress with a sharp tongue, and not too generous with the food she doled out, but she really couldn't be blamed for this.

Fred Humble had come for Eliza, just as he had done for Ada. It was no use worrying about it any more, they told themselves philosophically. What was done was done, and nothing they could say or do would make the slightest difference now.

Eliza Dodds had gone for good.

Towards the end of October, Harriet March arrived at Easton Mallet to take up her post as governess to Sir Valentine Easton's nephew, Jonathan.

She approached the village by way of a dirt-track, clinging to the side of the pony-trap as it jolted her uneasily over the uneven stones, glad when they reached Marsh Road and its smoother surface.

"That's Potters Piece ahead," said the carter, who lived some miles away but who knew every stick and stone of the surrounding countryside. "Some think it's the village

green when they first come upon it, but it ain't. There be
the real Green, over yonder."

The light was beginning to fade, but there was still enough
left for Harriet to note the various landmarks pointed out
to her. As they turned into Mill Road, she could see the
inn falling away behind them, and to their left the houses,
set well back from the road, half-concealed by trees.

"Pond House," said her guide and spat over the side of
the trap. "Miss Batsby lives there, and a right rum one she
be. Next is Lantern House, belongin' to Mrs. Drewhurst.
She be rich, they say, though not true gentry to my way of
thinkin'."

"And the thatched cottage over there, through the trees?"

Harriet sat upright on the uncomfortable seat, a small girl
of nineteen years, her corn-gold hair severely dressed beneath
a tiny black hat perched forward on her brow. Her complexion was as fine as porcelain; her eyes large and dark
amber in colour; her mouth full and pink like a morning
rose. The gown she wore was of black wool trimmed with
a row of tiny buttons down the front, a spotless white fichu
at the neck. Her jacket was grey plaid, her gloves plain black
cotton.

"That be Vine Cottage." The carter's tone was a clear
indication that he did not approve of its occupant. "Some
young gent from Lunnon; come 'ere to recover from an illness, it's said. Only seen 'im once or twice meself when I've
been deliverin' parcels, but 'e looks puny to me."

The trap followed the half-circle of Mill Road on one side
of the village green and began to make its way up Lords
Walk which led to Easton Hall. The carter, having done his
duty by his passenger, lapsed into silence, and Harriet was

left to make her own assessment of what she saw.

Easton Mallet lay in a shallow dip of land, some three miles from the Kentish coast. In the centre was the Green, its shops and nearby houses, and to the north Easton Hall, lying behind high walls and wrought-iron gates. Across the fields to the east was the church, with its old rambling rectory and dark, unkempt churchyard. To the south, past a dirt-road, was a wide field, with Parsons Pond in its centre, surrounded by stunted trees, whilst further south still, over Widders Walk, there was another meadow, with the cottages of the villagers spilling into it like a handful of rough stones.

Beyond the Hall was Helsketh's Farm, and at the opposite end of the village, well away from the bustle of Mill Road and the Green, was Chase Manor which, the carter had told Harriet, was the home of a widow of considerable means.

As the trap moved nearer to their destination, Harriet felt a sudden qualm. It was impossible to pin-point her disquiet, for there was really nothing about Easton Mallet to cause the slight chill which was running along her spine, nor the absurd impulse to order the carter to turn about and drive her back to Camley.

She chided herself for her foolishness. It was a perfectly ordinary country village, shared by farmworkers and their wives, and the more affluent people who lived in red-brick houses with neat, sparkling windows and painted front doors. Yet somehow she could not dismiss the sense of foreboding which had overcome her.

She told herself that it was merely nerves, and that the prospect of meeting her new employer was the real cause of her alarm. That the fading light was giving the village a sinister air which it did not really possess, and that when she saw it in daytime, she would laugh at her own folly. But her severe lecture to herself was in no way convincing. There were too many trees concealing the houses; too many paths and tracks leading off into nothingness; it was too secretive and self-contained. Finally she forced herself to ask a question.

"It seems a pleasant place," she said untruthfully. "Would you like to live here?"

The carter did not reply at first, and Harriet wondered if he had dozed off with the reins between his gnarled fingers, but then he gave a grunt.

"Not me, miss. I only comes 'ere to deliver, and to take a passenger now and then, such as yerself, but I wouldn't live 'ere."

"Why not?"

She knew instinctively that he did not want to answer, but she pressed him until his thick shoulders shrugged in resignation.

"Best not to talk of these things," he said at last, "but I'll tell yer this. I wouldn't spend a night 'ere whilst Fred 'Umble's about, not even if yer gave me a gold sovereign. I'd rather meet me Maker than 'im, and that's the truth of it."

Easton Hall lay back from the road some mile or more. Once through the gates there was still the long curving drive to negotiate before the house itself came into sight.

Harriet caught her breath as she stared up at its black outline against the evening sky. It was larger than she had imagined, with quirkish turrets and odd little steeples in

9

unexpected places. She had been told that the original house was very old, and doubtless that had been simple enough, but succeeding generations of Eastons had added to the structure until it had become a joke. Harriet wished she could have found the heart to laugh at the jest, but she couldn't. The Hall had the same unwelcoming, withdrawn air as the village itself, and as the door opened she almost backed away before her last chance to escape was gone.

Yet it was no ogre who received her, but a gaunt woman with iron-grey hair under a no-nonsense linen cap, whose keys rattling at the belt of her full skirt proclaimed her the housekeeper. She did not smile, contenting herself with a quick inspection of Harriet and her modest belongings, before she said briefly:

"In future, miss, you'll use the back door, same as we do. Your trunks can stay there; one of the men will bring them up later."

"Thank you." Harriet felt uncomfortable, as she was meant to do. "I am sorry that I came to the wrong door."

"No harm done. You'll know next time. This way."

The housekeeper led Harriet across the hall. Only a few gas-lamps were on, and the panelled walls and timbered ceiling were wreathed in shadows. There were a number of doors off the hall, but all were firmly closed as if shutting Harriet out just to teach her her place. They passed through an archway into the rear of the house, where a back stair-case led up to the second floor. It was cold and cheerless, with a half-hearted oil lamp here and there to light the way, and thin drugget underfoot.

After what seemed to Harriet an interminable time, they reached their destination.

"This is your room, miss," said the housekeeper, "next to Master Jonathan's, and there are three spare rooms besides."

When the gas-lamp was turned up, Harriet looked around her. It was a large room, with plain but good quality furniture, and an old but respectable carpet. The curtains were still drawn back, and there was a window-seat covered in cretonne, with bookcases in the alcoves and a solid oak table by the wall. Harriet was glad to see that there was a fireplace, even though it was innocent of coal or wood, and she laid her small valise on the bench at the foot of the bed and smiled in relief.

"It is a nice room. I had not expected to be given one so large."

"All the rooms in the Hall are large." The woman said it without pride; merely stating a fact. "I'm Mrs. Tate, the housekeeper. The others you'll meet later on."

"Are there many servants?"

"Not now." Mrs. Tate's mouth turned down at the corners. "The master doesn't live here normally; that is, he didn't do, until his brother died and he had to take Master Jonathan in. The boy's mother died years ago, you see. Then he came down here from London, about six months ago."

"How sad for Jonathan. What happened to his father?"

Mrs. Tate ignored the question.

"At the moment, there's Comper, the butler; Rawlston, the master's valet; Mrs. Grace, the cook, and the two maids, Heggarty and Pearce. There are the grooms, of course, and stable-boys, but they're no help to us in the house." She gave Harriet a straight look. "Speaking of which, miss, there had better be no misunderstanding between us. Less trouble for us all if it's said at the beginning."

11

Harriet's gaze had been on a heavy mirror over the fireplace, but at the sharp note in Mrs. Tate's voice she turned quickly.

"Yes?"

"Heggarty will bring you a jug of hot water every morning at six-thirty, and once a week she'll help you to fill the bath what's kept behind there." She nodded in the direction of a shabby screen with faded silk panels. "Apart from that, you'll have to wait on yourself, for we've no time for it."

Harriet nodded, keeping her slight grimace to herself. It was what she had expected, of course, for a governess lived in an unhappy limbo, not accepted as a member of the family, and a source of irritation to the servants, who were always at pains to make it clear that she was no better than they were, and warranted neither service nor favours from them.

"Of course." She said it meekly. "I quite understand."

"You'll have your evening meal in your room, and you can fetch your tray at eight o'clock from the kitchen. Breakfast and luncheon are different. They're served in the small dining-room for Master Jonathan, and you'll eat with him."

"Where is Jonathan?"

"Master Jonathan is not well. He's in bed."

"Oh? What is wrong?"

"A chill. No need for a fuss."

"Has the doctor seen him?"

Something passed over Mrs. Tate's face which Harriet almost missed. It was so quick and intangible that she thought she must have imagined it, but later she had cause to remember it.

"Sir Valentine will decide when he's to be called. It's no

12

business of yours or mine."

"May I see him?"

"Not to-night. The master will see you in the morning. Ten sharp, in his study."

"I meant Jonathan. May I see him? I won't disturb him."

"Likely as not he's asleep."

"I will not wake him."

Mrs. Tate opened her mouth to protest, but then her eyes met Harriet's. For a second neither spoke; then Mrs. Tate looked away. It was a small victory, but Harriet knew she would would have to pay for it.

"If you must. It's this way."

At the door of Jonathan's room, Harriet said firmly:

"There is no need for you to wait, Mrs. Tate. I know how busy you are, and I would not want to keep you from your duties. You may be assured that I shall not upset Jonathan."

"Well. . . ."

"And I will be down to fetch my tray in a short while."

Harriet slipped into the room and closed the door before Mrs. Tate could reply, listening for the retreating footsteps before crossing the floor to the bed. It was dark, only one candle burning on the bedside table, but she could see that the room was furnished in a manner similar to her own, with the same high windows and marble fireplace.

When she looked down at the bed, she found Jonathan Easton wide awake. He was a thin slip of a child of ten years, with a small triangle of a face devoid of colour, and hair the hue of a chestnut.

"I hope I did not startle you." She said it politely, smiling at him as she sat on the edge of the bed. "I'm Harriet March."

13

At first she thought he wasn't going to answer, but after a moment he nodded.

"I guessed you were. You've come to take Miss Bailey's place, haven't you?"

"She was your last governess?"

"Yes, but she ran away."

Harriet's smile did not fade, but inside she could feel the alarm tighten into knots again.

"Did she now? Why was that? Did you bully her?"

She made a joke of it, but Jonathan did not respond.

"Oh, no, it wasn't that. She was afraid."

"Of what?"

He did not answer, turning his head away so that he did not have to meet her eyes.

"Jonathan? What is it? Why was she afraid?"

"Because of what was happening, I suppose."

"But what was happening?" Harriet was torn between exasperation which she dared not show, and a growing sense of apprehension. Miss Bailey was not the only one to be afraid; Jonathan Easton was equally frightened. It was clear from the pallor of his face and the way his small fingers clutched at the bedclothes, as if they afforded him some protection from whatever it was that he dreaded. "Come, sweet, it couldn't have been that bad."

"Yes it was." He turned his head again to look at her, refusing to let her dismiss his terror so lightly. "It was, Miss March. You see, she saw the hearse one night, and the man in the churchyard."

Harriet felt her mouth dry slightly, but she gave no sign of her consternation.

"Hearse? You mean someone died and there was a

14

funeral?"

"No, no one died. The hearse comes at night, you see. Not often, but now and then." He sat up and hugged his knees, his blue eyes fixed on hers. "I've not seen it, of course, because I'm not allowed to go out at night, but I've heard Heggarty and Pearce talk about it. It's all black, they say, drawn by two horses with plumes and silver bridles."

"But that's absurd; they must have been mistaken."

"No, no, they're not. Others have seen it too."

"But where does it come from?"

"No one knows, nor where it goes."

Harriet felt a strange helplessness as she stared at the child's worried face. She wanted to put her arms round him and comfort him, but it was too soon. She would have to earn the right to do that, and it would take time.

"And the man in the churchyard?"

Jonathan gave a small shiver.

"Oh, him. That's Fred Humble; everyone knows that. Whenever he's seen, we know something bad is going to happen."

Harriet sat by the window in her room and looked out at the darkened garden. She had not been able to get any more out of Jonathan Easton, and since it was clear that the child was unwell, she had not pressed him.

After she had tucked him up and bade him good-night, she had gone to the kitchen to fetch her supper tray. The servants had already started their meal, and they looked up from their plates to stare at her with mixed curiosity and hostility. Comper, silver-haired and neatly dressed; Mrs. Grace, a good advertisement for her own cooking; Heggarty, the

15

younger maid, brown-haired and stocky; Pearce, tall, willowy with dreamy eyes; Rawlston, the valet, small, well-groomed with a bald pate.

Her tray was waiting for her on the white-wood dresser, and Harriet had murmured her thanks and beaten a hasty retreat. She was an intruder, and she could feel eyes boring into her back as she hurried up the stairs to the second floor.

When she had eaten her meal she unpacked, and then took her seat by the window. It was beginning to get chilly, but there had been no suggestion of laying a fire in the grate, and so she had wrapped her shawl about her shoulders, lighting both oil-lamps to supplement the one gasolier by the door.

It was not an encouraging beginning. The servants were more unfriendly than she had expected, and her small charge was unwell and obviously frightened. It would take some time to gain his confidence, and doubtless he expected her to turn tail and run like the unfortunate Miss Bailey.

It only remained now for her to meet her employer, Valentine Easton. He had engaged her as a result of a letter sent in response to his advertisement, and his reply had been brief and business-like, giving no indication of the man himself. She guessed that he would be old, for this was an old man's house. Although she had not seen the main part of it, the servants' quarters and the second-floor were enough to tell her that.

She wondered if Sir Valentine knew that his nephew spoke of a hearse seen at night, and of a man called Fred Humble, who roamed the churchyard. If she could pluck up courage in the morning she would ask him, but then she pulled a face. Perhaps it would be unwise to do that, for she did not

16

want to lose her newly-gained position, and he might well send her packing if she mentioned such nonsense.

But was it nonsense? Slowly Harriet got up and opened the purse lying on her bed, pulling out a letter and staring at the envelope for a long while. Then she went back to the window-seat and read it again.

It was from Kate Plum, who had been in service in the London house where Harriet had lived for the last few years. Kate had been a round, rosy girl, full of fun and undaunted by the grinding work which kept her on her feet from five-thirty in the morning until eleven o'clock at night. Kate never grumbled. She said that she had her health and strength and an assurance of God's mercy, and that was as much as anyone could expect out of life.

When her widowed mother died, Kate had had to return to Easton Mallet to take care of her younger brothers and sisters. She had not wanted to go but, as she had said sadly to Harriet, it was her duty and there was no choice. Two of her brothers were just old enough to work in the fields, and Kate herself helped one of the farmer's wives, and somehow there was just enough money to keep the family alive and to put a handful of coal in the grate of a winter's time. For two years, Kate and Harriet had corresponded: not often, but enough to keep the link between them unbroken. Kate's letters, badly written and full of spelling mistakes, were cheerful and courageous, that is, until the last one.

Harriet unfolded it reluctantly. It was the kind of letter which should have been read in a roomful of people, with plenty of bright lights, not in the gloom of an October night with no one but a scared child anywhere nearby.

17

Kate began without preamble to relate the disappearance of her cousin, Eliza Dodds. Eliza was an orphan, said Kate, and since her mistress didn't give her enough food to keep a bird alive, Kate had somehow managed to make her own meagre rations stretch far enough to give Eliza a good hot dinner now and then.

Despite her lack of scholarship, Kate contrived to make the story spring into swift and ugly reality. The first realisation that the girl had gone; the slow-thinking, but good-hearted, men setting out on their search; their return, empty-handed, shaking their heads; Kate's own tears which had stained the paper on which she had written.

"You see, miss," wrote Kate, "the village ain't what it was. Something has happened to it. Blessed if I can explain it rightly, but it's just different. Eliza weren't the first to go, and there's other things besides, like the lights what are seen in the churchyard at night when no one's there.

"Sometimes I think it's because of some who've come to live 'ere lately, for when I was a girl, there was nothing like this. The village was peaceful then; now it's disturbed, and won't rest.

"Have I told you, miss, about the woman who talks to the dead? They calls her a medium, though I don't exactly know what they mean by that. Her name's Batsby, and she holds them seeances. Sinful, I calls it. No wonder things 'ave gone wrong, for we weren't meant to call back the dead. People come from London to see her now and then, and others, here in the village, go to her too. She don't hold them things in 'er own home, but in Lantern House, where Mrs. Drewhurst lives. I don't like Mrs. Drewhurst. Even the widow goes sometimes. They say awful things about 'er and

18

Sir Valentine, but I'm not one to repeat gossip, so less said about that the better."

Harriet looked up. So Valentine Easton was not beyond an illicit relationship, even if he was advancing in years. She wondered why he didn't marry the widow and stop the talk, but perhaps she wasn't that sort of woman.

"But if only I could find Eliza, I wouldn't mind about the rest of it. She were so young, you see, and a lively little thing. I can't bear to think of what might of happened to her, 'specially if Fred Humble has got her. Oh, miss, if only I could see you and talk to you about it, I wouldn't feel so bad."

Harriet folded the letter up and put it away. She had read it many times since it had arrived a month ago, and it still made her want to weep. When Valentine Easton's advertisement for a governess had appeared so soon after the letter, it had seemed more of a nudge from Fate than a coincidence, and she had not hesitated to write, praying that she would get the post so that she could be close to Kate to offer her some comfort.

And now she was here at Easton Hall. Rather nervous, and not looking forward to her interview in the study at ten o'clock on the following morning, but at least there, and not more than a mile or so away from Kate's cottage. Somehow, to-morrow, she would beg an hour of freedom and go and see Kate, and then perhaps she could find out more about the mystery of Eliza's disappearance, and the elusive man who hid in the churchyard after dark, lying in wait for young and innocent servant girls.

At ten o'clock precisely on the following morning, Harriet

tapped gently on the door of the study and was bidden to
enter.

As she went in she was conscious of several things crowd-
ing in upon her at the same time. First, the room itself was
not at all what she had expected. She had thought to find
it dusty and shabby, but it was bright with the sunlight flood-
ing through the windows; mahogany furniture polished to
mellow loveliness. There were comfortable leather chairs,
and bowls of flowers, with a large desk furnished with silver
and crystal inkstand and pen tray. Handsome oil-paintings
in heavy gold frames hung on the walls, and there were tall
glass-fronted bookcases in the recesses by the fireplace.

Only when she had digested this did Harriet look at the
man by the window. As she did so, her sense of shock
deepened, and she could feel all the colour recede from her
face.

Valentine Easton was as far from her mental picture of
him as it was possible for any man to be. He was well over
six-foot, dressed in immaculate riding habit, still holding a
crop in his hand. His hair was dark and slightly curled, and
he had the deepest blue eyes Harriet had ever seen. His face
was lean, but the bones beneath the lightly tanned skin were
excellent; his nose thin and high-bridged, giving him a look
of arrogance; his mouth well-shaped but set in hard lines.
When he moved, it was with a powerful kind of grace, as
if the expensive clothes he wore hid a latent force kept under
careful control. He could not have been more than thirty or
so, and Harriet's lips parted in mute astonishment.

"Miss March?"

His voice was soft, but Harriet did not mistake its quality,
and she nodded quickly, wishing that there had been some

way of knowing in advance what manner of man Easton was. He made her feel almost gauche and awkward as he motioned her to sit down, and she could hear the breathlessness of her own voice as she replied.

"Yes, I am Harriet March."

"I am glad you are here. You know that my nephew is unwell?"

"Yes. I saw him last night."

He gave her a quick look.

"Did you? What did you think of him?"

"I thought him a nice child. He seemed...."

"Yes?"

She was going to say that she thought Jonathan had been afraid, but the disconcerting blue eyes were on hers, and she could not bring herself to get the words out.

"I thought him rather feverish."

"Yes, he will have to stay in bed for a day or two. Meanwhile, your time is your own. Look round the village; see what you make of it."

"Thank you." It was more than she had dared to hope for, for now she would be able to visit Kate and spend as long as she liked with her, but her sense of duty made her hesitate. "What about Jonathan? Should I not stay to look after him?"

"It is not necessary. Mrs. Tate will do that. He's a quiet child, you'll find; very withdrawn."

"Perhaps he misses his father."

The thin black brows met in a slight frown.

"Perhaps."

She was put firmly in her place; it was not for her to ask questions about Easton's dead brother.

21

"The last woman couldn't handle him. He was always running away from her. In the end, she ran away herself."

"Yes, Jonathan told me. He said she was afraid."

Valentine eyed her silently for a moment. Then he shrugged.

"I doubt that. She had probably had enough of Jonathan. And are you comfortable in your room?"

"Thank you, yes. It is so much larger than I expected, but Mrs. Tate says all the rooms are big."

"They are. It is an impossible house, and I have always avoided using it, but now. . . ." He broke off abruptly. "There is one thing, Miss March, of which I must warn you."

"Yes?"

"There is a door at the end of your corridor which leads to the west turret. It is locked, and in no circumstances are you to go into that part of the house. It has become unsafe, and you could be hurt."

"I will remember."

"Do so; I want no accidents."

He said it so curtly that Harriet felt as though he had slapped her, but then his expression changed as he looked over her shoulder.

"Michael, come and meet Jonathan's new governess. Miss March, Michael Paris."

Harriet rose to greet the newcomer in silence. He was of the same age as Easton, slim, lithe and impeccably dressed, smoking a thin, expensive cigar. She thought him almost as good-looking as Easton, with hair the colour of sable, and hazel eyes.

Paris let his gaze travel slowly over her, pausing as he

reached her face, a small smile touching the corners of his mouth.

"Lucky Jonathan," he said softly. "I was never as fortunate in my youth. How is he this morning?"

"The same." Valentine was swinging his crop slowly back and forth. "I have told Miss March that she is free to do as she likes until he is well enough for his lessons."

"Do you know Easton Mallet?" Paris sank gracefully into an armchair and tilted an eyebrow at Harriet. "I find it a somewhat limiting place myself."

"No." Harriet hesitated. "No, I have not been here before, but I have heard things about it."

She only just caught the swift look which the two men exchanged, but it made her heart miss a sudden beat. The faint amusement had gone out of Michael Paris's face, and Valentine's mouth had taken on a new harshness.

"Have you, indeed? What, may I ask?"

She paused again, not quite sure how to answer Easton's question, but he was obviously waiting for a reply and so she said quickly:

"Well, I was told some odd things have been happening here."

"Odd? In what way?"

"Well, that lights have been seen in the churchyard, and that a hearse appears sometimes after dark."

"Good God, you do not believe that rubbish, do you?"

Easton was short, but in spite of that Harriet had the distinct impression that he was relieved. Whatever he had expected her to say, it was not concerned with hearses and lights, and she said slowly:

"No, no, I don't think I do, but Jonathan said. . . ."

23

Paris gave a quiet laugh.

"Don't believe what Jonathan says, Miss March. He listens to the servants' gossip, and that, as you may imagine, is never reliable."

"The carter who brought me here said something too."

"Once a rumour like that starts it is hard to stop it." Easton was growing tired of the subject, flicking his whip impatiently against the side of the desk. "I advise you to put such things out of your mind, and do not encourage Jonathan to talk of them either. He is prone to nightmares as it is."

She flushed. "Of course I shall not talk to him about such things, but if he is worrying about them. . . ."

"See that he is kept busy with other things."

Clearly the interview was over, and Easton said coolly:

"I hope you will stay, Miss March, despite these absurd tales. This is a lonely place, and I do not have time to. . . ." He broke off again. "Jonathan wants company, and he needs some sort of education before he goes away to school. Fill his head with tables and history, not with phantoms."

She could feel the warmth on her cheeks again, glad to escape from the study. Easton and Paris were so unexpected, that she had been caught totally off-guard. They must have thought her a simpleton, and perhaps Easton was already regretting the fact that he had employed her to teach his sensitive young nephew. A girl who believed wild stories about hearses!

She wondered why Easton had returned to the village, since he clearly disliked the house and was totally out of place in such a quiet backwater. He could easily have taken Jonathan to his London home, but instead he had chosen

24

to bury himself in the country with a companion as sophisticated as himself.

As she put on her jacket and bonnet she thought again about the look which Easton had exchanged with Paris. It had been brief, but significant, and she worried about it whilst she drew on her gloves.

Two handsome and very worldly young men, who had elected to live in a remote village, and who had something to hide which obviously had no connection with bucolic fantasies.

Harriet stared at her reflection in the mirror, smoothing a strand of hair into place, the feeling of doubt increasing as another question slid into her mind.

If it was not the tale of the hearse which had made them look at one another like that, what was it?

TWO

Harriet March left Easton Hall at about ten thirty. She knew that Kate Plum would not have returned from her work at Helsketh's Farm until mid-day, and so the whole morning stretched before her, an oasis of blessed freedom.

The sun and the crisp freshness of the morning lifted her spirits as she made her way down the drive and through the gates into Lords Walk. There was nothing ominous about her journey that day. On each side, the fields were shorn and stubbly after the harvesting of the wheat, and here and there clusters of small cottages broke up the emptiness.

There were a number of people gathered outside the row of shops facing the Green; village women in their plain, linsey-woolsey dresses with shawls over their shoulders, and long white aprons, with a man or two in serviceable smocks, corduroy breeches and bright spotted neckerchiefs. There was a cobbler's shop which looked dark inside, smelling of leather even as one passed the open door; a grocery, and a general store with pots and pans, brooms and brushes and a few rolls of coloured cloth crammed into its tiny window.

Harriet went into Mr. Tyght's shop, braving the stares of the women who were eager to see the master's new governess, smiling at them rather shyly as she purchased some tea, sugar, flour and bacon, for if she were to visit Kate,

26

some small offering would not come amiss in that hard-pressed household.

When the grocer had parcelled up the goods, Harriet made her way to Potters Piece and sat on the fallen trunk of a tree. It was still too early to call on Kate, but she felt a strange contentment, sitting in the sun, laughing inwardly at her fears of the previous night.

When she heard the sudden canter of horse's hooves she look up quickly, shading her eyes from the light. The rider slowed down as Harriet stood up and stared at the woman on the chestnut mare with a mane as fine as silk.

Harriet thought she was the most beautiful woman she had ever seen, even in the severity of the black riding habit. Her dark hair was pulled away from the perfect oval of her face, faint colour touching the high cheekbones and breaking the lovely pallor of her complexion. She had eyes like slanting jet stones and a mouth as red as a strawberry. For a few seconds she looked down at Harriet, not smiling, but assessing her as if she were an enemy whose potential danger had to be measured with care. Then she struck her mount with her whip and was gone.

Harriet sat down again, her legs suddenly and unaccountably weak. She had no doubt as to the identity of the woman. It was the widow of Chase Manor, whose name she yet had to learn; the woman whom Kate said was linked with Valentine Easton by sly rumour and innuendo.

After a while Harriet pushed the whole incident out of her mind. It was no business of hers whether her employer had a mistress, nor whether that mistress was so exquisite that it almost hurt to look at her. It was something to be dismissed, and in any event it was now time to go and see

Kate.

Kate Plum came to the door of her cottage, the tears running down her cheeks as she saw Harriet.

"Oh, Miss Harriet, Miss Harriet! I'm that glad to see you."

Harriet's own voice was not quite steady as she took Kate's work-worn hands in hers, but soon the moment of emotion was over and Kate was ushering Harriet into the cottage. It was a tiny place, with two rooms on the ground floor and two above, supplemented by a decrepit shed at the rear. The floor was plain wood, scrubbed almost white, with a simple wool rug in front of the fire, and a table and benches by the window. Apart from a dresser filled with oddments of china, and a wheezy old clock on the wall, there was nothing else but a single cheap print in a tarnished gilt frame over the mantelpiece.

When Kate had chided Harriet for bringing the food, smiling in delight as she began to make tea in a chipped brown pot, they sat together by the fire and sipped the strong, sweet liquid.

"Children won't be back yet," said Kate thankfully. "I loves 'em, of course, but it's a real treat to 'ave this hour to meself." She looked at Harriet with affection. "I couldn't believe it when I 'eard you was coming to the 'All. Why did you do it, miss?"

Harriet laughed softly. "To be near you, of course. I was lucky to get the job. I haven't had much experience, as you know."

"But. . . ."

"Enough of me." Harriet was firm. "Your letter worried me, and I was so sad to hear about Eliza. You have heard

28

nothing more, I suppose?"

"No. We shan't 'ear any more now. She's gone."

"There was so much that you didn't tell me. Kate, what is going on here?"

Kate shrugged, not meeting Harriet's eye. Harriet regarded her thoughtfully. Kate had lost weight, and the fresh, youthful look had gone. She was no more than nineteen or so, but already she looked years older, with strain painting smudges under tired eyes, and dragging down the corners of her mouth.

"I reelly don't know. It's like I told you in the letter; things have changed."

"Lights in the churchyard? And what is this about a hearse? Kate, people must have imagined these things."

"I don't think so. More than one 'ave seen 'em, and folks around 'ere aren't given to imagination. No, there's an 'earse all right."

"But where does it come from? Where is it seen?"

"Here and there; not always in the same place. As to where it comes from . . . no one knows."

"It is too silly!" Harriet was tart because she had to make Kate see that the hearse was no more than an hallucination. "You can't truly believe that it is . . . well . . . that it is. . . ."

"Real, miss?" Kate looked up with a forlorn smile. "I didn't think so at first. I thought, like you, that it was just a story made up by some to scare others. Now I don't."

Harriet bit her lip. "You said things had changed since others came to live here. Whom do you mean? The widow?"

"Mrs. Lester? No, I don't think she has anything to do with this. We don't see much of 'er. Now and then we see 'er out riding, but she don't have anything to do with the likes of us."

"Only with Sir Valentine."

Harriet's tone was sour, and Kate gave her a pensive look. "So they say, miss."

"Well, if it is not she, who is it?"

"It may not be any of 'em, but after Miss Batsby came 'ere and started them . . . them seeances. . . ."

"Séances? Kate, do you really mean to tell me that in a place like this, this woman holds séances? It is incredible."

"Maybe, but she does. I've never been to one meself, of course, for I don't 'old with such goings on, but others encourage 'er, and it stands to reason that the dead don't like to be disturbed."

"And this Mrs. Drewhurst. What about her?"

"She come 'ere two years back. She's a widow, too, though not like Mrs. Lester. Stout, she is, and gettin' on in years. Got money too."

"But you don't like her. Why not, Kate?"

"Can't say." Kate got up and refilled their mugs. "She's done me no 'arm and I don't see much of 'er. Once or twice I've done a bit of cleanin' for 'er, when 'er maids 'ave been sick or away visitin' their folk. 'Er place is a regular little palace, miss, and she paid me well, but. . . ."

"But?"

"But she makes me uncomfortable. Always seems to be watchin' me somehow. Can't explain it proper."

Harriet dismissed Mrs. Drewhurst for the moment and stirred her tea.

"The carter who brought me here mentioned a young man. I think he said the boy had been ill."

"Oh, that's Mr. Carrington; lives at Vine Cottage on the other side of the Green. Nervous as a kitten, 'e is."

"Could he have anything to do with what is happening?"

"Don't see 'ow. 'E doesn't go out much, you see. Keeps 'imself to 'imself."

"What do the doctor and rector think of all this?" Harriet felt a sense of helplessness as she looked at Kate's pinched face. The whole story was so fantastic, and there were no solid facts to get a grip on. "Surely they tell the villagers how ridiculous it all is?"

Kate's mouth twisted slightly. "Dr. Sawyer ain't much interested, miss. He's got other things on 'is mind."

"What sort of things?"

"I shouldn't say."

"You should, Kate, to me, at least."

Kate hesitated, then sighed.

"Well, I suppose you'll 'ear about it soon enough. 'E drinks, you see."

Harriet stared at her. "Drinks?"

"Yes, miss. No one talks of it openly, of course, but everyone knows about it."

"I see."

Harriet frowned. No wonder Easton had not called upon Sawyer to attend Jonathan. She tried again.

"Well, the rector then. What about him?"

"Mr. Long?" Kate looked at Harriet sadly. " 'E's as poor as a church mouse. A quiet man, and a kindly one, I've no doubt, but 'e's no match for this."

"But doesn't he try to talk to people about it? To show them how wrong it is to believe in such things?"

31

"No, 'e doesn't talk much at all. Some say 'e's hidin' something, for 'e doesn't mix much, if you know what I mean. Stays up at the rectory most of the time."

"And Lucy Morton? What about her? Eliza worked for her, and so did the other girl you mentioned."

"Ada? Yes, that's true, but she couldn't be responsible. Neat as a new pin, she is, and works 'ard, but there's no charity in 'er and that's a fact. She goes to them seeances though."

"Does she now? Who else goes?"

"Mr. Carrington sometimes, and some of the farmers' wives, who ought to know better. Then there are them who come from farther off, of course."

"I think I shall have to attend one too."

"Miss Harriet! You can't!"

Kate was shocked, her eyes startled as she shook her head violently against such a notion.

"But I must. There has to be some reason for all these foolish rumours, and since they have not long started, and as Miss Batsby has not been here for many months, there may well be a connection. After all, who else is left?"

Kate sighed deeply.

"No one, I suppose, 'cept those up at the 'All."

Harriet grew very still, keeping her hands tightly round the cup in case their unsteadiness should alert Kate.

"The Hall?"

"The master's not been back long either, miss."

"Surely you don't think that Sir Valentine or Mr. Paris could have had anything to do with it. Oh, Kate, how could they have?"

Kate shook her head again.

"No, I suppose not. People whisper things now and then,

but I don't suppose it means much. It's not as though 'e lived 'ere all 'is life, you see. 'E's almost a stranger to folk hereabouts. Some seem almost afraid of 'im."

"Without cause, I am sure," returned Harriet briskly, and with more assurance than she felt. "He is quite civil, you know."

"Maybe, miss, but 'e goes out a lot at night."

Harriet's chin tilted a mere fraction.

"Perhaps to visit Mrs. Lester."

"Perhaps."

Harriet changed the subject abruptly, not quite sure why she was so anxious to thrust aside the subject of Valentine Easton and his widow.

"The thing I find most puzzling," she said, putting her cup down, "is why no one tries to find this man Fred Humble. If the men know who it is who took Eliza and Ada, why don't they go after him? It is obvious that he is not far away, since he's been seen in the churchyard. He may not be responsible for the hearse, but it is clear enough that he took the girls. Why don't they catch him?"

Kate's face was bleached of colour and her fingers were gripped together until the knuckles stood out bone-white.

"You . . . you don't understand. They can't do that."

"Why not? Surely. . . ."

"No, no, it isn't possible, Miss Harriet. You see, Fred Humble is dead. He died over a year ago."

Imogen Batsby came out of church on the following Sunday morning and opened her umbrella. It had been raining since dawn, and the sky was grey and sullen overhead. She was a thin woman, with faded blonde hair puffed out into rolls at the back of her head, and light eyes under sandy lashes. Time had creased furrows on her brow and drawn ugly lines from her sharp nose to the corners of her small mouth, and she seemed to hold herself in, as if she were afraid that someone might stretch out a hand and touch her.

She went to church every Sunday, although she knew God would never listen to her prayers whilst she continued with her work, but she had to try. She had to make Him see how desperate she was, even if she could not stop doing the things which were making Him so angry. Victorian England had taken spiritualism to its bosom, and none with more fervour than Imogen, who was convinced she had a true gift. She had enjoyed that side of her life in the discreet villa in Battersea, that is, until things began to go wrong. She pushed some of her fears aside to consider one in particular, for that was pressing hardest on her at the moment.

She could still remember the day on which Mrs. Smith had come to see her. Mrs. Smith was a very ordinary woman, quiet and plainly dressed. She sat through the séance, and listened to what Imogen had said to her about ridding herself of a burden which was ruining her life. Then she had paid her fee and bidden Imogen good-bye and Imogen had forgotten her until she read the papers a week later. Mrs. Smith had been arrested for the murder of her crippled and imbecile son, and on the day that she was hanged, Imogen had found a note thrust through her letter-box. It was signed by James Smith, threatening her life because of the rubbish she had told his wife which had landed her on the gallows.

It had been time to leave London in any event, and Imogen was glad to go, but the fear went with her. Sometimes it lay dormant for a month or more; then it would spring to life again, and she would begin to imagine that James Smith had found her. She was sure about it now, as she moistened her lips and walked down the path to join the two women by the lych-gate. As she reached them, Bertha Drewhurst turned and smiled.

"Ah, Miss Batsby, we were just talking about you."

Imogen looked at Mrs. Drewhurst nervously. She was a well-proportioned woman in her fifties, smartly-dressed in a gown of twilled shot-silk under a long jacket of good wool cloth. A tiny feathered and ribboned hat perched on her russet-brown hair, and her dark eyes were bright and speculative.

"Were you?"

"Yes, indeed. This is Miss March from the Hall. She's Master Jonathan's new governess, and I've been telling her all about you. She's most interested." Mrs. Drewhurst looked at Harriet with approval. "Have you ever been to a séance before, Miss March?"

"No." Harriet could see the dread in Imogen Batsby, but she pretended not to notice it. "No, I haven't, but I would love to do so, for I've heard so much about them."

"Then you must come to my house on Wednesday afternoon, for Miss Batsby is to sit for us then. She's going to try to get in touch with that poor girl. We feel it's the least that we can do."

"Poor girl?" Harriet shot her a look. "You mean Eliza Dodds?"

"That's the one. I expect you've heard all about it, although you've only just arrived. News travels fast in a place like this, for there's not much else to talk about."

"You think she is dead then?"

35

"Certain to be." Mrs. Drewhurst was very definite about it. "What else could have happened? If she was alive, someone would have found her by now."

Harriet gave a small, contrived laugh.

"I'd heard that Fred Humble had taken her."

"That's just the villagers talking, my dear; you don't want to take any notice of them. Fred Humble's dead, you know. A terrible thing, really. He was buried alive."

"What!"

Harriet could not stop the exclamation. She had not pressed Kate for further details of Humble, for Kate had been too upset at the time to make sense, and she was unprepared for Mrs. Drewhurst's startling announcement.

"Oh, yes, it's true enough. He was a farmhand. Got a fever of some kind and was gone in two days, or so they thought. Quite a nice funeral it was, with his poor wife weeping as they took him up to the churchyard in a wagon."

"But how. . . ."

"It was two months after the burial that grave-robbers came to Easton Church. There's a lot of it going on, you know." Mrs. Drewhurst said it darkly and shook her head. "They get a good price for bodies not long buried, you see. Anyway, they opened poor Fred's coffin but something must have disturbed them for they ran off. It was then that people realised Fred had been alive when the lid was nailed down. All the signs were there, and, after all, we're always reading about such things in the papers, aren't we?"

Harriet felt queasy, but Mrs. Drewhurst was right. Premature burial, or at least certification of death, was by no means an uncommon thing, and when there was no more interesting news item to be found, the papers thundered furiously against the carelessness of the medical profession in their haste to get rid of their patients.

"Who ... that is ... who. ..."

"Dr. Sawyer, of course. Poor man, he's not been the same since it happened."

"But do the villagers think Humble is still alive?"

Mrs. Drewhurst chuckled.

"No, no, they're sure he's dead now, but they think he's turned spiteful. They say he's making people pay for what happened to him, and that's why they think he took those girls." She turned to Imogen Batsby with a bright smile. "But Miss Batsby will prove it isn't so, won't you, my dear?"

Imogen murmured something inaudible, but then Mrs. Drewhurst's pony and trap arrived to take her home, and Harriet was left alone as Miss Batsby made a brief excuse and scurried away.

Harriet was about to follow them, when she thought she heard a sound behind her. She turned quickly, peering through the drizzle, but there was nothing to be seen. She could feel her heart pumping with unnatural vigour, but she told herself that she was a fool, and to punish herself for letting her imagination run away with her, she turned back into the churchyard.

It was a place to be avoided, even on a June morning when the sun was high. On a wet autumnal day, it was grey and eerie, with a dank depression hanging over it like a pall. It stretched a long way back from the road, too full of trees with gnarled and twisted trunks, dotted with headstones which looked like crooked teeth sunk into tall grasses and weeds. Here and there was a pool of water, stagnant and slimy, and everything about it smelt of death and decay.

Harriet's shoes were getting sodden with water, and the hem of her skirt flapped miserably about her ankles, but she forced herself to go on. Finally, the disused mortuary chapel came into sight, old and crumbling and hunched up on the far edge of the churchyard. Harriet paused. There was really no need to go any further. It was clear that there was no one about, and that the sound she had heard must have been the flutter of a bird's wings in the bushes, or perhaps a rabbit making for its burrow. Besides, the rain was getting heavier, beating down in a silver sheet before her eyes. It was pointless to go on, simply to prove that she was not afraid of ghosts.

It was then that she saw him. He moved from behind a clump of trees, passing only momentarily within her sight, and then he was gone. Harriet was shaking in every limb, and she hardly knew how she stumbled back over the rough earth, bumping into a headstone now and then as she rushed for the lych-gate.

As she made her way back to Easton Hall, she told herself that she had been mistaken. What possible reason could he have had for being in the churchyard, for he had not been at the service, of that she was certain. Yet in the brief second that she had seen him, there had been no doubt in her mind. Tall, dark-haired, broad of shoulder, moving with that unmistakable grace which she had noticed when they had first met. No, she couldn't have been wrong, but what had Valentine Easton been doing there, and why had he run away?

Margaret Lester finished her luncheon leisurely and told her maid, Horton, to clear the table. Then she went to the drawing-room window and watched the rain falling in a steady downpour, her mouth drooping in discontent.

She had gone to church that morning, mostly to alleviate the boredom of the day, rather than because she had any personal conviction in the efficacy of prayer or the necessity for worship, but she had not stayed to chatter to anyone after the service and had got quickly into her brougham and ordered Horace to drive off.

She had no time for the vulgar Mrs. Drewhurst and refused to acknowledge her whenever she could, and although now and then she attended séances at Lantern House, simply to lighten the tedium of life, she saw no reason to be pleasant either to Bertha Drewhurst or the peculiar Imogen Batsby when they met on other occasions.

The governess from the Hall had been there too. Margaret had noticed her at once, sitting quietly in one of the back pews. She wondered if the girl realised how beautiful she was, with her thick corn-coloured hair and eyes like jewels. Probably not, but undoubtedly Valentine would have done so. Her lips compressed in anger. Easton seemed to be avoiding her lately, and it was time she reminded him that she was not prepared to accept such treatment. Time to draw his attention to the relationship which they had had in London, when he had been attentive, passionate, and apparently jealous if she so much as looked in the direction of another man.

She sat down at a small bureau and pulled a sheet of paper towards her. She would ask him to dinner, in such a way that he could not refuse. God knows it was not much to ask of him; a few hours of his time. Damn him! Why did she have to beg? She would make him pay for his indifference when he came. If he wouldn't come willingly, then he could come unwillingly; it made no odds. But come he would, for she knew something about Easton which he would not want others to discover, and the price of her silence would have to be paid no matter how much he resented it.

Imogen Batsby finished the over-cooked lamb chop and mashed potatoes and pushed her plate away. She had given her maid, Lotty, the day off, for she wanted to be alone to think.

Pond House sounded important, but it wasn't. It was really no more than a cottage, with a front parlour, a slip of a dining-room and a kitchen, with three cupboard-like bedrooms above.

She had first come across Easton Mallet when she was on her way to the coast, and she had been instantly attracted by its solitude. She had had to leave London, and had decided to move near to the sea, but when she had seen the village and found that Pond House was for sale, she had looked no further. Now, of course, it was different. She would have given anything to have got away, but it was too late. She would have to stay now, and the cottage had become nothing more than a prison.

Wearily she took the dirty plate into the kitchen and left it for Lotty to deal with on her return. Everything was very quiet, only the steady rain breaking the silence. She found herself listening again, waiting for another sound, but nothing came. She took a book and sat by the fire, unable to concentrate on the words, letting her gaze roam round the parlour. It was so cosy, with chintz at the windows and an Axminster carpet on the floor. Lotty kept the furniture polished until it shone, and her mother's china looked well on the shelves on each side of the fireplace, yet she was beginning to hate the place.

Then she heard it, and the book fell to the floor as Imogen got unsteadily to her feet. She knew it must be him, for who else would be rattling her letter-box at that time of day? He was trying to get in, as he had tried so often in the last month or two. She wanted to scream and tell him to go away. To shout at him, and to defend herself against his accusations. How was she to have known that his wife would kill their mad and crippled son? She had not even known the woman had a son, and certainly she had not expected her to take a knife and cut the boy's throat. How could she possibly have anticipated that?

Somehow she reached the hall. She knew that she would have to face him sooner or later, and desperation made her fumble with the lock and wrench the door open. The rain beat in at her, splattering her skirt, the wind chilling her hands and face.

Then slowly she shut the door. He had gone again, perhaps not yet ready to make an end of her. Drearily she went back to the parlour and picked up her book. At least she was safe for the moment; he wouldn't come back that day. She could relax now until Lotty returned to make supper for her. Maybe, as she'd tried to face him at last, he wouldn't come back at all.

She shivered and buried her face in her hands. Oh, God; why didn't he go away? Why didn't they all go away and leave her alone?"

41

Percival Long stared at his reflection in the dusty mirror over the sideboard. Everything in the room was shabby and old, like the rectory itself, but nowadays he hardly noticed things like that.

He could see nothing in the gaunt creature in the glass to remind him of the eager young curate who had started out with so high a heart and such a fervour of love for God and his fellow man. It had all drained away somewhere, although he was not quite sure when or how. When he had accepted the benefice of Easton, he had known that he would go no further. Easton was the kind of living where men were quietly forgotten.

He hadn't minded really, despite the small stipend and even smaller congregation. At first, he had been quite happy with his books, glad to have escaped from a parish in the slums of Manchester to the beauty of a Kentish village. Now, of course, it was different.

He looked down at his hands and found that they were shaking. He tried to scourge himself with contempt for his own cowardice, but it was no good. Here, in the solitude of his own dining-room, he might as well admit it. He was afraid.

He had been afraid from the first moment he had seen the man in the churchyard. It was not the kind of fear that he was used to; concern for his lonely old age, lack of money, God's wrath at his failure as a priest. No, this was quite different: a kind of raw terror, which made his mouth dry and his bowels turn to water. He knew that he should have dismissed at once the primitive panic which the sight of the man had aroused in him. He should have rationalised and reasoned and pushed off the lunatic possibility that the villagers' tale of Fred Humble was true. But he hadn't been able to do it. What he had seen, he had seen, and now he could not bring himself to go out of the house after dark, at least, not into the churchyard. Whatever it was that was out there, it was evil, and he could not find in himself the courage to meet the Devil on those terms.

He sat down at the table again, feeling drained and exhausted. That girl who had lingered behind after the service had seen something too. He had watched her through the window as she had fled blindly through the gate as if Satan were snapping at her heels. Of course, there was some excuse for her: she was a woman and young at that. There was no such excuse for him. Sooner or later he would have to go out again at night and face whatever it was that was there. If he didn't, the time would come when he would no longer be able to face God either.

Harriet went to bed early on Sunday night. Jonathan was better and sleeping quietly when she looked in on him. She stopped in the corridor for a moment, looking both ways. It was a lonely part of the house, for the servants' quarters were on the other side, and only she and Jonathan slept in the west wing.

She thrust the thought of such isolation out of her mind as she got into bed and began to read, but her mind was too full of other things to concentrate. She thought it might help if she were to marshal her thoughts into some kind of order, so that she could face the facts squarely and dismiss the nonsense.

The story of Humble was dreadful, of course, but the man was dead now, and unless one were foolish enough to believe in ghosts there was no possibility that he had been responsible for the disappearance of Eliza or Ada Mullins. The hearse and the lights in the chapel were difficult to explain, but collective hallucinations were not unheard of. There were many cases on record of a group of people swearing on oath that they had seen some totally impossible happening, and Easton Mallet, after dark, lent itself to such illusions.

But if commonsense was to be the master, as surely it must be, what had happened to the two girls? Could they both have run away to make a better life for themselves? Kate had sworn that Eliza would not do such a thing, for she had been a loving child and would never have caused her family such worry. Certainly there had been no apparent preparations on her part for flight. All she had taken with her was a basket containing a few of her own home-made biscuits for her cousins.

And then there remained the incident in the churchyard that morning. Why should Valentine Easton have been there, and could there be any connection between his odd behaviour and the fact that Eliza and Ada had vanished?

Harriet was about to consider this unpleasant possibility in more detail when she heard the sound of voices. At first, she thought it was two of the servants who had come over to her wing for some purpose, but when she got up and opened the door, there was no sign of anyone. The voices were louder, one raised in violent anger, and at that precise moment she turned her head and saw the door to the west turret close very slowly. Then the voices were stilled, and Harriet was left to face the silence once more.

She could feel herself shivering, and was turning back to

her room when she became aware that Jonathan was crying and hurried in to him. She found him huddled under the blankets, his face blanched, his small nose pink and moist.

"Did you hear them?" He sat up and reached for her hand. "Miss March, did you hear?"

"The voices?" She forced herself to be calm. "Yes, I heard them. I suppose it was the servants."

"No, they sleep on the other side of the house. They never come here at night."

"But who else could it be? Your uncle?"

"No." The boy's face clouded. "No, he doesn't come here either."

"But it must have been someone. Who else . . . ?"

"It's not them. I know it's not them. I've heard the voices before; shouting and angry."

"I'll talk to your uncle about it in the morning."

"He won't listen. I tried once, but he said I was imagining things."

"I'll try anyway."

Jonathan moved closer, and she could feel the warmth of him against her body. After a moment or two she ventured an arm round his shoulders, and when it was not rejected, pulled him nearer, holding him tightly until he had stopped shaking.

"If I tell you something, Miss March," he said finally, "you won't say I'm imagining things, too, will you?"

"It depends what you say." Harriet kept her tone light, for the danger was not quite over and the boy's eyes were still suspiciously bright. "What is it?"

He studied her face for a moment; then he said slowly:

"I think there's something awful in the west turret."

45

Harriet froze inside, but she used every ounce of her self-control to stop herself stiffening so that Jonathan should not be alarmed again.

"But it's empty." She said it firmly, trying not to remember the sight of the heavy oak door swinging shut. "Your uncle said it wasn't safe."

"I know, but I still think there's something there. I think that's where the voices come from."

"It can't be so, Jonathan." She denied the possibility quickly. "What could it be?"

"I don't know." The boy's voice dropped to a whisper. "I can't think, Miss March, unless, of course, it's Fred Humble."

THREE

Harriet found Valentine Easton in the morning room. She was not sure how to broach the subject, for something told her he would be sceptical or angry, but it had to be done.

"My dear Miss March," he said when she had finished, "do you really expect me to believe what you are saying?"

"Yes, I do." She held her ground, determined to make him listen. "There were voices; loud voices. I was not the only one who heard them. Jonathan did too, and he was frightened."

"I told you that Jonathan had nightmares."

"But I do not, particularly when I am awake."

"Then you suffer from a lively imagination."

"I can assure you, Sir Valentine, that I do not. Why should I imagine voices?"

"I have no idea." He lay back in his chair and studied her coolly. "All I can tell you is that you are in error. There is no one in that part of the house except you and the boy."

"What about the turret?"

His blue eyes were cold and hostile.

"What about it?"

"I saw the door closing as I went out into the passage."

His face was expressionless as he reached for a letter and began to open it with a silver paper-knife.

47

"That seems improbable, since the door is locked."

"Is it?"

"Oh, I am sure you know that it is, Miss March," he returned suavely. "Have you not tried the handle?"

She coloured, and he nodded.

"I thought so. I told you to keep away from the turret. Some of the ceilings are unsafe."

"But the voices. . . ."

"You were mistaken." He paused to read the letter as if she were not there. Then he laid it down on the desk with a faint sigh. "I hope you are not going to encourage Jonathan in his silliness. It is time he grew up. I had hoped that you would help him to do so."

Harriet ground her teeth, but she knew she had reached a dead-end and so she changed the course of her attack.

"May I ask, Sir Valentine, why you were in the churchyard yesterday morning, and why you ran away when you saw me?"

She saw the expression in his eyes and almost backed away. Then it was gone as quickly as it had come, and he gave a thin, humourless smile.

"More tricks of the mind, Miss March? I was not in the churchyard yesterday morning."

"I saw you. You were running between the trees."

"My dear girl, I am not given to such violent exercise, particularly in the pouring rain. What on earth would I be doing in the churchyard?"

"I do not know. That is why I asked."

She could see the lines round his mouth and the hardening of his jaw, knowing that he was lying, but equally certain that he had no intention of confessing it.

48

"I was here yesterday morning, with Mr. Paris. You may ask him if you wish, but I must make one thing plain." He sat up suddenly, and his voice was very definite. "It is no business of yours where I am at any given time, and if I tell you that I was not in the churchyard yesterday, I expect you to believe me. Furthermore, I am concerned to find that you are harbouring these fancies; I thought you more sensible. If you cannot put them out of your mind, you will be no use to Jonathan."

Harriet knew she had to make a choice. She could press her accusations, in which case he would turn her out and she would have no chance to discovering why Eliza had gone, nor would she be able to protect Jonathan. The alternative was to apologise and beat a hasty retreat. She chose the latter, for Jonathan could not be left on his own to face whatever was happening.

Later, when she had recovered some of her poise, she went for a walk in the grounds. After a while she found herself by the stables, listening to the soft whinnying of tne horses and smelling the warm odour of hay and manure. She was aware of the sound of the stable-hands some distance away, but thought herself alone apart from them. It was an unpleasant shock when she heard Michael Paris's voice, and she drew closer to the side of the barn, not intending to eavesdrop, but waiting for a chance to run.

"You will have to be more careful, Valentine." Paris's drawl was quite soft, but it carried in the still air. "The girl is not a fool."

"I know that." Easton was brief, but she could hear the irritation in him. "But it is none of her business."

"She may try to make it so."

"Then I shall get rid of her."

Paris laughed quietly, but there was no amusement in him.

"A third girl disappearing so soon might be too much, even for this benighted place."

Easton said something which Harriet could not catch, and then the two men moved off. She leaned against the barn, wishing she were anywhere in the world but there. She tried to tell herself that she had misunderstood what she had heard, but it was no use. Why should Michael Paris mention Eliza and Ada, unless Easton had had something to do with their going? Besides, he had said Easton would have to be more careful, and Easton himself had lied about yesterday morning.

Somehow she got back to the house and went slowly upstairs to her room, startled when she met Rawlston on the landing. He looked as spruce as ever, and nodded to her, but his eyes slid away from hers quickly as he made for the stairs. She almost called him back to ask what he had been doing, but that might have made things worse, and she had had enough rebukes from Valentine Easton for one day.

"Has Rawlston been to see you?" she asked Jonathan when she went in to see him. "I have just met him on the stairs."

Jonathan was heavy-eyed, his face hot and flushed.

"No, but Uncle Valentine came."

"Oh?" She looked at him quickly. "Did you tell him what happened last night?"

"I was going to, but he already knew. He was angry with me, and said I was old enough to know better." The blue eyes were suddenly full of tears. "I don't think he likes me very much, Miss March. I'm a burden, you see."

Harriet was silent for a moment, quietly hating Easton. Then she said slowly:

"I'm sure you're wrong. Why should he dislike you?"

"Perhaps because of my father."

"But. . . ."

"I don't think Uncle Valentine liked him either. He will never talk to me about him."

"How . . . that is . . . how did your father die?" She did not want to upset the boy any more, but she had the oddest feeling that her question was important. "What happened to him?"

Jonathan's small face crumpled in misery as he shook his head.

"I don't know; Uncle won't tell me. He says it is better that I shouldn't know. Oh, Miss March, do you think he could have been murdered?"

On Wednesday afternoon at five o'clock, Mrs. Drewhurst's visitors were settling down in her parlour. The room was large, with windows along one wall, now covered by heavy drapes of prune-coloured velvet. It was a sombre place, for all the luxury of the thick carpet and solid, comfortable chairs, lending itself admirably to the purpose for which the small group had gathered there.

Lucy Morton took her place at the round oak table and let her gaze wander cautiously about her. She was only shown into the parlour on the occasions of the séances: when she visited Lantern House to help with the household sewing, or to make a gown for Mrs. Drewhurst, the linen-room was considered quite good enough for her. She let her resentment smoulder for a second or two, but then other emotions chased it away.

She glanced across the table at the girl from the Hall, her mouth compressing in an unconscious anger. The bloom on the girl's skin was an affront, for it mocked Lucy's own advancing years, and her hair was so thick and glossy that Lucy wanted to tear it from her head. She hated the governess already, although they had not yet spoken to one another, just as she had hated Eliza Dodds and Ada Mullins. They had both been young and pretty too. Ignorant and common, of course, and nothing more than peasants, but their eyes had been clear and innocent, their cheeks pink and glowing with health. She had made them pay for their young beauty, working them hard from early morning until late at night, but even when fatigue made them droop and drained their faces of colour, they were still pretty creatures, and she loathed them for it.

Margaret Lester took her place a few minutes later, rustling in expensive silk and smelling of a rich, musky perfume. She was inclined to scoff at herself for attending the séances, for they were really too ridiculous, and much of what happened was faked, yet they held some queer fascination for her which she could not clearly define, and in any event filled in an empty hour or two before dinner.

Alastair Carrington was already in his place, a lock of dark hair falling over his brow. He carefully avoided meeting anyone's eye, for then he might have to talk to them, and that he did not want to do. He told himself that it was his illness which had made him want to avoid human contact, but deep inside himself he knew that wasn't true. He had always avoided people when he could, only studying them when he was sure they were unaware of him.

He took a furtive look round. It was the same old crowd. Mrs. Trout, the doctor's chatterbox of a housekeeper, smiling and smug in her new green dress and jet beads; Mrs. Lester, hard and untouchable, and somehow repulsive with her air of superiority and faint, scornful smile; Lucy Morton, prim, proper, tight-mouthed and growing dry and shrivelled in middle-age; a couple of farmers' wives, as fat and bovine as their husbands' cows, and Taylor, the maid, who was privileged to join the circle.

It was then that he noticed the newcomer, and he could feel something run through him like the beginning of a fever. He had been told that there was a new governess at the Hall and that she was going to join Mrs. Drewhurst's guests, but he had not thought for a moment that she would be so lovely. Perhaps rather too old; nineteen or so at least, but still youthful enough to make the palms of his hands sweat as he hid them under the table.

He could not remember when he first realised that he had a craving for young girls. Not like the governess on the opposite side of the table, but like Ada Mullins and Eliza Dodds, with their sweet innocence and budding womanhood which made him writhe inside until he was sick with frustration. He had been in the habit of following Ada, when her mistress sent her on some errand or other, keeping a discreet distance and totally absorbed in the way her body moved as she bounced along. He knew that she was scarcely more than a child, and that what he wanted to do to her was wrong, but he couldn't help it. He lay awake at nights, picturing Ada stripped of her shabby cotton dress and apron and her long black stockings, savouring the thought of her round white thighs and small breasts. He knew too that he wanted to hurt her before he made love to her, and he had often taken out the leather strap he kept locked away in his bedside cupboard, running it lovingly through his hands. After Ada, Eliza had caught his fancy, but then, in no time at all, she had gone too.

He gave a shuddering sigh, wishing the séance would begin so that the thoughts he was beginning to harbour for the new governess could be kept in decent check until the time was ripe to let them have their head.

At ten minutes past five, Mrs. Drewhurst and Imogen Batsby appeared, and Taylor turned down the gasoliers, leaving the room lit by a single candle. The spirits did not like light, so Mrs. Drewhurst said, and darkness was essential if any communication was to be made.

Harriet scolded herself for the slight quiver which ran through her as the gas-lamps went out. It was all a lot of nonsense, of course, and she had only come to learn what she could about Eliza, and perhaps something more about her employer. It was absurd to imagine that Imogen Batsby could communicate with Eliza, or anyone else for that matter, yet as the murmur of voices was stilled and Miss Batsby bade them spread their hands on the table, their outstretched fingers touching their neighbours, Harriet was oddly apprehensive.

At first, there was nothing to see except the pale blur of Imogen's face, but after a moment Harriet became aware of a strong smell of flowers, almost overpowering, and reminding her unaccountably of a graveyard. She shook herself mentally. She was being a fool. She had graveyards on the brain, and there was no sense in associating them with the essence which clearly had been allowed to leak from a small phial, probably in Miss Batsby's pocket. But when she looked back at the table, her lips parted and she felt the tremor again. If it was a trick, it had been done most cleverly, for no one had appeared to move, and yet there, spread before her, were newly-cut flowers, moist and fresh, as if the dew had just fallen on them.

Before she could gather her wits, lights began to appear; pale fluorescent blobs, darting about the room like eerie dragonflies. She heard someone moan, and Mrs. Drewhurst's quick demand for silence, but then her whole attention was on the burst of music above her head, as she twisted away to avoid what looked like the outline of a guitar. There was a cry from her left as a tambourine flew across the table, and Harriet could feel the heavy table rock slightly as if someone were tilting it. She took a quick look round, the distant candle just sufficient to show that the circle of hands was still unbroken. It had to be a ruse. Miss Batsby was shifting the table with her knee, or perhaps her foot, yet the table was so heavy and Imogen Batsby appeared to be unconscious.

It had grown very cold, and the candle was flickering as if a wind were passing through the room. When it went out, one of the women gave a faint scream, and Mrs. Drewhurst said sharply:

"Hush! No sound please. Any noise now could injure Miss Batsby in the most terrible way. Please be very quiet."

The deathly silence dragged on for a moment or two longer, the cold increasing until Harriet could feel her skin covered with goose-pimples. Just as she thought she would have to move, no matter the consequences to Miss Batsby, there was a rustle and someone said:

"I am here."

It was a childish voice, and Harriet strained her eyes in the blackness but it was no use. She could see nothing, and she sat very still, waiting for more.

"I'm Eliza." The voice sounded quite close, a clear treble blurred by the local dialect with which Harriet was becoming familiar. "I've been waiting to come to tell you what happened."

A quick shudder went round the table. Harriet could sense it, as if it was travelling through the linked fingers, jarring her nerves and rattling her determination to remain cool and detached. It was left to Mrs. Drewhurst to ask the questions, which she did with practised composure.

"We are pleased that you are here, Eliza. People have been worried about you."

"Did they miss me?"

"Of course."

"I'm glad. It would be sad not to be missed."

"Where are you, Eliza?"

"It's hard to say."

"Are you still here? On earth, I mean."

"Oh, no."

"Can you tell us what happened to you? A search was made, but the men could find nothing."

Eliza's voice dissolved into a giggle which sent a tingle down Harriet's spine.

"No, they wouldn't, would they? I wasn't there."

"Then where were you?"

"In Calder Mere, of course. I fell in."

There was a whisper of understanding from the listeners, but Harriet frowned. She had not heard of Calder Mere

56

before, but assumed it to be a lake of some kind. She wished the séance would finish quickly, for her arms were growing numb, and she was becoming increasingly sleepy in spite of the cold air which was blowing through the room.

"You drowned in Calder Mere?"

There was no reply and Mrs. Drewhurst repeated the question, but still without response.

Harriet was not sure what happened next, for it seemed to her that for a brief second or two she herself fell asleep. The next thing she was aware of was a room fully lit, and Miss Batsby stirring and asking Mrs. Drewhurst anxiously if anything had happened.

Soon hot tea was served, and Harriet drank hers gratefully, listening silently to the conversation of the others.

"Well, that is that." Mrs. Drewhurst crooked her little finger elegantly as she sipped her tea. "The poor child was drowned. No wonder the men couldn't find her. They say Calder Mere is bottomless."

"Then it weren't Fred Humble," said Mrs. Smallwood, one of the farmer's wives. "I allus thought 'e 'ad taken 'er."

"And I." Her companion's normally florid face was pasty-white. "Poor mite, but what was she doin' as far off as Calder Mere? That's a tidy step away."

"She used to go off." Mrs. Smallwood shook her head. "Often I seen her wanderin' away. Not looked after proper to my way of thinkin'."

Lucy Morton's pinched face turned in the speaker's direction.

"If you mean that I did not care for my servants, I can assure you that you are wrong. I was always telling the girl not to go beyond the village, but she was headstrong and wouldn't heed me."

Margaret Lester looked at Lucy Morton with derision.
To listen to the woman one would think she had a full staff
of servants, instead of one wretched maid-of-all work whom
she had bullied unmercifully. She said idly:

"Perhaps she had a lover."

There was a swift gasp of disapproval, and heads turned
to her in reproof. None of them really liked the widow, yet
there was a certain excitement in having her present, because
one was never sure what kind of shocking thing she was
going to say, and there was always the chance that she
might let something slip which would give a further clue to
her relationship with Valentine Easton.

"She was too young for that," said Mrs. Drewhurst after
a moment. "She was only a child."

"Hardly." Margaret's dark eyes flickered over her hostess's face. "What was she? Fourteen? Fifteen?"

"Fourteen, and. . . ."

"That is quite old enough, I can assure you."

Lucy Morton caught her breath. The woman was quite
outrageous with her blatant immorality. How she dared
appear in public, Lucy could not think, since everyone knew
that she was Sir Valentine's mistress. Bitter gall rose in
Lucy's throat. She had never been any man's mistress, and
never would be now. She hated Margaret Lester for her
satisfied self-assurance, wishing she could slap the beautiful
face which was like a mask, devoid of lines or wrinkles.

Alastair Carrington said nothing. He was remembering
the evening in question and praying that his thoughts did
not show. He had seen Eliza as she left the house, twinkling
along in spite of the heavy boots on her slender feet. He had

58

taken another route through the village, but had come upon her later, sweating slightly as the girl bent to tie her boot-lace, watching breathlessly the slim ankle and the beginning of a plump calf. He couldn't remember any more, or perhaps he didn't want to. He was not quite sure which it was, but he thrust the whole thing out of his mind and forced himself to listen to Mrs. Drewhurst.

"Well, my dears, that is an end to it. Poor thing, it was a sad end for her, but we can put her cousin's mind at rest and stop some of these foolish speculations we've been hearing lately."

"You mean about this man Humble?"

Bertha glanced at Margaret Lester.

"They're only silly tales." Bertha did not like the widow any more than anyone else did, but there was a certain cachet in having her at Lantern House. She was definitely a woman of breeding, no matter that her morals left a lot to be desired, and it would not be wise to offend her. "I would take no notice of what is said if I were you."

"Oh, but I should love to meet Fred Humble." Mrs. Lester's teeth were pearl-white against her red lips. "I should find him most entertaining, I am sure."

Imogen Batsby put down her tea-cup, feeling the strength begin to flow back into her veins. She had no idea what had happened when she had fallen into a trance, but it appeared that she had met with some success, because Mrs. Drewhurst was beaming at her with undisguised approval. Imogen gave a small, unseen shudder and looked away.

She was hardly aware of the others, now talking together round the table. She was not jealous of the widow's beauty, nor of the loveliness of the girl from the Hall. If she had any envy at all, it was for the farmers' wives and their slow, untroubled lives, safely tucked away in the old houses lying out in the meadow. They were the lucky ones; they had nothing to fear at all.

She got stiffly to her feet.

"I think I shall go home now," she said and gave Mrs. Drewhurst a funny little bow. "I'm feeling rather tired."

"Of course, my dear, of course." Mrs. Drewhurst was all concern, bustling up and calling to Taylor to fetch Imogen's wrap. "We are grateful to you; all of us. Now you go home and have a good rest. You deserve it."

Harriet made her excuses too, anxious to be away, particularly from Margaret Lester. As she put her coat on, she found herself thinking about Valentine Easton and the widow, and was amazed at the strength of her emotions. It was no business of hers what Easton did, and she could well understand why he found Margaret Lester so attractive, but what she could not fathom was her own distaste for the notion of their relationship.

She began to walk back to the Hall with a grim determination not to think of either of them again for the rest of the evening. Night had fallen, and the trees seemed to have moved closer. She began to hurry, wishing she had left Lantern House earlier before the light had gone completely.

As she passed the corner of the village green and turned into Lords Walk, Alastair Carrington moved out from behind an oak, quickening his pace as he fell into step a cautious distance behind her.

At eight o'clock on the following evening, Valentine Easton called at Chase Manor. He gave his cloak and hat to Horton, ignoring the woman's arch and conspiratorial glance, and went into the drawing-room.

Margaret Lester rose from the chair by the fire and held out her hand.

"Valentine, how good to see you. I thought you had quite forgotten me."

He touched the tips of her fingers with his lips, but did not return her smile.

"I have been busy," he said shortly. "I told you that when I left London, I should not be able to see much of you."

"I do not see why." Her gaze was faintly hostile. "I thought your reasons stupid. I still do."

"I am not in the least interested in your views on the subject, my dear Margaret," he returned coldly. "For God's sake use your intelligence. This is not Belgravia. We should have everyone whispering about us in no time at all."

"They are whispering already." Margaret's flash of irritation at his tone was snuffed out by a purr of satisfaction. "Do you really suppose that the yokels are ignorant of the truth about us? Oh come, you are not that naïve."

"So be it, but there is no point in making matters worse. I shall not be staying here for ever. Can't you exercise some patience?"

"I could, but I don't choose to do so." She poured him a generous whisky and sat down again. "Come, my love, don't sulk. We have little enough time together as it is."

"I am not sulking; don't be absurd."

He sat opposite her, as angry with himself as he was with her. Once, he had found her irresistible, and had not cared who had known that they were lovers. Now, there were other things of far greater importance to think about, and, in his present position, Margaret was a threat.

He studied her over the rim of his glass, wondering why he had thought himself so much in love. She was beautiful, certainly, but it was rather an artificial kind of beauty: Margaret was as cold and hard as the diamonds which she wore on her breast.

"Is Michael still with you?"

"Yes."

"How odd that he should want to bury himself here." She was feline and full of secret knowledge. "So unlike Michael."

A muscle at the corner of Valentine's mouth twitched. She was probing at something, and he would have to be careful.

"Do you think so? I find nothing odd about it myself. Easton Mallet is a pleasant place in which to spend the autumn."

She gave a caustic laugh.

"It is a ghastly place in which to spend any season, and you know it."

"Then why are you here?"

"Because of you, of course. I told you that I would follow you. I was fortunate to find a house so close to you."

Her eyes taunted him during the brief silence; then Valentine said tautly:

"I think you should go back to London."

She regarded him from under half-closed lids, the smile still on her mouth.

"Do you now? But I am not going, you know. I did not follow you here to be turned away so easily."

"In God's name, why did you follow me?"

She laughed, glad to have stung him into some show of

emotion.

"You know why. It is because I love you, and want to marry you."

"That is impossible; I've told you so before."

"I didn't accept your answer then and I don't now. You will come round to my way of thinking in time."

"Indeed I shall not. Go back to London, Margaret, I don't want you here."

Her smile faded at last and there was something ugly in the depths of her dark eyes.

"Damn you, Valentine. I won't let you reject me like this."

"You have no choice. Go home."

The passion died and she moistened her lips with the tip of her tongue.

"You're wrong, you know."

"What about?"

"I have a choice. It is you who lacks that luxury."

"Oh?" The blue eyes were frigid but his tone was cautious. "Why is that?"

"You know why. Oh come, sweet, don't pretend with me. There is no need for that."

"I have no idea what you are talking about."

"Yes you have; you know exactly what I mean. These villagers may have some bizarre explanations for what is happening here at Easton Mallet, but I know the truth. Did you imagine that I didn't?"

She could feel his withdrawal, almost afraid when she saw the look on his face, but she had gone too far to give up now.

"What are you saying? Are you referring to these ludicrous stories about hearses and lights in the churchyard?"

"Amongst other things." She smiled again in an attempt to stop her lips betraying a quiver of alarm, for there was something about Valentine's stillness which was quite terrifying. "And then there are the missing girls, of course. I went to a séance yesterday."

He made no reply, and she went on quickly.

"That peculiar woman, Batsby, went into a trance, or it was said that she did. Probably it was a lie. Anyway, there was a voice, not a bit like Batsby's. It sounded like a child, or someone quite young. It, the voice I mean, said she was Eliza, the girl who disappeared. She claimed that she had drowned in Calder Mere, but I don't think she did, do you?"

"Why do you ask me?"

"Because I think you know, Valentine."

There was another silence, more strained than the last, then Margaret said hurriedly:

"There is no need for you to be afraid."

"I'm not."

His words were mild enough, but there was an underlying menace which made her draw back.

"If we were as we were before, there would be nothing at all for you to worry about. You know that I would not say a word to anyone, and would lie for you, if I had to."

"There is nothing to lie about, and we are not as we were before, nor ever will be again."

She got up abruptly, her face flushed as if he had struck her .

"You are not being very wise, Valentine, are you? I could do you a great deal of harm; you know that."

He said nothing for a long moment. Then he put his glass aside and stood up, too, looking down at her.

"I don't think you could, Margaret," he said very softly. "Whatever you know, or think you know, could be as great a risk to you as it is to me. Have you stopped to think about that?"

He saw a pulse move in her temple and raised one hand to touch her cheek.

"Poor Margaret."

"What do you mean, poor Margaret? Why. . . ."

"I mean that if you really do know something, then you stand in considerable danger." His strong, thin hand moved suddenly and closed gently about her throat. "I do not like being blackmailed. You've chosen the wrong man, my dear."

His fingers tightened momentarily. Then he let her go, and she swallowed convulsively.

She had no time to speak, for Horton was opening the door to announce that dinner was served, and Valentine proffered his arm.

"How opportune," he said silkily, and watched her hand tremble on his sleeve. "I think we have both had enough of melodrama for one evening, don't you?"

"You . . . you will stay afterwards?"

She had been shaken by what she had seen in him, but with Horton close by some of her self-possession had returned, and she still wanted him with every fibre of her being, despite the fact that a moment before he had chilled her to a deathly coldness.

"Do you want me to?" He glanced at her again, his eyes calm once more. "How very brave of you, Margaret, but after all, why not?"

FOUR

Two days later, Samuel Forest woke at two o'clock in the morning to the sound of his daughter's screams.

Samuel, one of Farmer Helsketh's hands, occupied Glebe Cottage, a tiny dwelling on the outskirts of the village. It was not much of a structure, but Samuel had made the most of it, keeping its thatched roof in sound order and its walls fresh with whitewash.

When Samuel reached Rosie and had shaken the hysteria out of her, his face mottled to an angry purple.

"What's that you say, girl? A man in yer room? You be dreamin'. Who'd want to do that?"

"I weren't dreamin', father." Rosie had a mass of tumbled fair hair and a skin like a ripe peach. "He were there, I tell you."

"But 'ow did him get in?" Samuel thrust past her into her room, his jaw clamping tightly as he saw the open window. "Through there, you reckon?"

"I don't know." Rosie was sniffing, but she knew better than to start screaming again, for Samuel had no time for women's weaknesses, and was likely to give her a box on the ear were she to annoy him further. "I just woke up, see, and there 'e was."

"Well, who was it?"

Forest was eyeing her with brooding concern. Bringing up the lively Rosie had not been easy, especially since his wife died four years back. More than once he'd had to wallop her backside because she'd been late home of a night, or because he suspected she was meeting some local boy against his instructions. He sometimes wished he'd had a plain daughter, for then his troubles would have been halved. As it was, Rosie was a sight for sore eyes, and Samuel turned his head away so that he should not have to look at the outlines of her nubile young body under the thin nightgown.

"If you've bin messin' with that Thomas boy," he began threateningly, "I'll take the hide off you. Didn't I tell you. . . ."

"Pa, it weren't him, I swear it weren't him. I'd 'ave known."

"No doubt you would, you little strumpet." Samuel glowered at her. "I've a mind to. . . ."

"It weren't him, I tells you. I don't know 'oo it were, but it wasn't Joe Thomas."

"Get back to yer bed," said Samuel finally, giving Rosie the benefit of the doubt. "I'll see about this in the mornin', and God 'elp the man when I finds 'im." He gave his daughter a black look. "You do bring this on yerself, and likely as not you've given this man the eye, flauntin' yerself at 'im until 'e couldn't stand it no longer. I've not bin strict enough, I can see that, but I'll mend that too in the future, never you fear."

Rosie flounced back to her room, but not too openly, for her father had a heavy hand, and she cried herself to sleep, partly because of the injustice of life, and partly because the dark shape of a man in the outline of the window had genuinely frightened her.

Next day, Samuel Forest began his enquiries with a truculent air. Getting leave of absence from Farmer Helsketh, who had daughters of his own, Samuel made his way to his neighbours' cottages to ask a few pertinent questions. He met with concern, sympathy, outrage, and pity, but no solution as to the identity of the intruder. Not deterred by early failure, he went on to the village and began to make enquiries there.

The women he spoke to all swore that their husbands and sons had been abed like Christian folk, a few of them giving Samuel the length of their tongue for suggesting otherwise, others shaking their heads as he went on his way, whispering together that Rosie Forest was no better than she ought to be, and that it was no wonder that something like this had happened.

When Forest met Percival Long, he stopped him to relate his tale. Long paled, taking a step back from the bellicose Samuel, wishing he had chosen another time to come to the village general store.

"I . . . I . . . don't know what to say, Mr. Forest." Long was always very formal with his parishioners. "It must have been a very upsetting experience for your daughter."

"Aye, and for me too." Forest was puzzled by the fear he saw in Long, but it was unlikely that the weedy parson would have had the agility to reach Rosie's window, or that he would have known what to do had he got there. "One of them fool women back there says it was Fred Humble, but for my money this one was of flesh and blood. I've no time for them silly tales meself."

He waited for Long to concur, his hot brown eyes narrowing as no such agreement was forthcoming, but he shrugged off the puzzle, having no more time to waste on the rector, and went on his way.

When he came upon William Sawyer he stopped to tell his story again. Samuel did not suspect for one moment that the doctor had had any part in the intrusion of Rosie's privacy, for like as not the doctor had been half-seas over, but, after all, he was a medical man, and Forest still had the countryman's almost superstitious respect for those who could cure sickness.

Sawyer was a heavy man, running to fat, with grey hair and a full beard. He half-listened to Forest, wishing the man would go away so that he could take a nip from his pocket flask to clear his head. It ached intolerably, but not so much as his heart. He had thought that when he came to Easton Mallet he would have a bit of peace. A few injuries to attend to; a childbirth now and then; the dying to help out of this world. The thought of the dying made him sweat anew, and he tried to focus on Forest, not because he was interested in the man and his whore of a daughter, but because it was better than thinking of Fred Humble. Finally, he had to get away.

"I am sorry sir," he said with as much firmness as he could muster. "I can think of no one who would violate your daughter in this way. Are you sure she wasn't dreaming? Young gels do have these fancies, you know."

"If I thought she were 'avin' me on, I'd make 'er sorry she'd been born," said Forest grimly, "but I don't think she were. She were real frightened this time. Well, thanks for yer time, doctor."

He touched his forelock and walked on, leaving Sawyer

fumbling in his pocket for his flask.

When he met Alastair Carrington crossing the Green, Samuel hesitated. He had not spoken to Carrington before, although once or twice he had seen him in the village. A sickly boy, he'd thought him, and not much good for anything, but after all, one never knew.

Alastair concealed his fear as he listened to Forest. He thought the man impudent, even to address him, never mind burden him with his problems, but since he could scarcely turn and run away, he was forced to affect some interest. As Samuel got under way, Carrington found himself suddenly absorbed. He didn't remember seeing the labourer's daughter, but it sounded as if she were young and pretty. He ventured a question or two, and Samuel grunted.

"Aye, I suppose she's fair enough. Only fifteen, mind, and needs a firm 'and. Thank your lucky stars you've no daughters to bring up, sir; they're a tidy 'andful, I can tell you."

"I'm sure you know what to do." Carrington was beginning to enjoy himself, willing Forest to go into details which he could dwell on at his leisure. "I am certain that you see she is obedient."

"I does me best." Forest was warming to Carrington's obvious sympathy. "She be a proper madam, and no mistake, but she knows better than to go too far with me."

"Of course. She would not want a lecture from you, would she? That would be too painful for any girl."

Forest looked at Carrington dubiously. He wasn't sure what a lecture was, but he made the position plain at once.

"If she don't do what I says, and be quick about it, she gets a tanning."

70

"I see." Alastair felt the excitement rise in his blood, craving more information. "Well, I suppose mild discipline does no harm."

Forest spat on the ground. He was beginning to think his first assessment of Carrington had been right.

"She gets more than that, master. When she come 'ome late not long since, I made sure she didn't sit comfortable for a week. Well, I'm sorry to 'ave taken yer time. I just thought yer might 'ave heard something."

Carrington walked on smiling to himself. Rosie would be worth knowing. Fifteen years old and fair enough. Even her father had said that, and he was probably under-estimating the girl's charms. The thought of her made him tremble, just as he had trembled for Ada and Eliza. Now that he had lost them, perhaps Rosie could take their place.

On the same day that Rosie Forest claimed a man had been in her room, Harriet found Jonathan white and shaky as he sat up in bed and whispered his morning greeting.

Harriet was shocked by his appearance, wondering at first if his fever had grown worse, but when she felt his forehead it was cool enough. Indeed, his hands were like ice when they touched hers, and she sat on the bed and looked at him with troubled eyes.

"What is it, sweet?" she asked gently. "Did you have another bad dream?"

"It wasn't a dream, Miss March." He seemed glad to have her there, keeping one of his hands in hers. "It was real."

"What was? What happened?"

"You'll be cross with me." He said it doubtfully, his eyes heavy with lack of sleep and something else which made

71

Harriet frown. "You'll say I shouldn't have got out of bed."

"Well, I don't think I'll be very cross this time. Hardly at all, in fact." She smiled reassuringly. "So you got out of bed. What then?"

"I thought I heard something outside and I opened the door."

The child seemed to shrink within himself, and his fingers tightened on hers. She was very calm and practical, for hysteria was not far away.

"Go on; what did you see?"

"Nothing at first, but when I went outside and walked down the passage towards the stairs, then . . . then. . . . I looked down at the landing and I saw him. Oh, Miss March, I saw him!"

She hugged him tightly until he had stopped crying, wiping his face with her handkerchief which smelt of cologne. Then she said:

"Who was it, Jonathan? One of the servants?"

"No. I told you: they never come here."

"Rawlston did." She said it half to herself. "Then who was it?"

"I don't know. He was tall, I could tell that even though it was dark, but he moved so quickly that I couldn't see anything else."

"Could it have been your uncle?"

"I'm sure it wasn't. If it had been, he would have spoken to me, not run away."

Harriet was not so sure that Jonathan was right about that, but his obvious distress made her bold enough to beard Easton in his study again later that morning.

"You are very persistent, Miss March."

She could see his expression under his bland exterior, but the thought of Jonathan's small white face spurred her on.

"Yes, I am. Jonathan was very frightened, and this concerns me."

"And me, but I cannot think that when you encourage him like this you are really helping him. You are something of a disappointment, Miss March. He seems to have grown worse since you arrived."

She was as angry as he was, and made no bones about it.

"It has nothing to do with my arrival, Sir Valentine, and if you are honest you will admit it. First voices, then someone on the landing! Are you really saying that these things are my fault?"

"I am saying that they have not happened at all," he returned briefly. "Now, if there is nothing else. . . ."

"I want to go into the west turret."

She said it baldly, waiting for his terse refusal. Instead, he gave her a faint smile.

"Oh, yes, you are persistent, aren't you? Very well, I'll take you in myself this afternoon. I will come to your room at three o'clock."

Harriet was so taken aback by her easy victory that she forgot the rest of the questions she had been going to ask, and hurried back to Jonathan, but three o'clock found her ready and waiting for Easton when he tapped on her door.

"We shall have to be careful," he said as he unlocked the door. "Follow me and watch how you step; there are some loose floorboards."

The turret was dark, but Easton had brought a lantern with him and Harriet was able to see the narrow treads of the stairs which led up to the main floor. There were only three rooms and, as Easton had said, they were in bad condition, with fallen plaster and odd pieces of wood lying about the place. There were small windows let into the thickness of the walls, and far below, Harriet could see the lawn like a green handkerchief bordered with gay colours.

"Have you see enough?"

Easton was leaning against the wall watching her, and she felt her colour rise in embarrassment. She had made a complete fool of herself, and if he had dismissed her on the spot, it would have been no more than she deserved. She had been so sure that someone was in the turret that her desire to inspect it had become an obsession. Now that she could see it was empty, there was nothing left to do but to apologise again.

"I am sorry." She said it quietly, looking at him squarely. "I was quite wrong in what I believed, but I was so sure. . . ."

"I am sure that you meant well." He sounded almost amused. "But I am glad that you are satisfied."

"Do you want me to go?"

"I hardly think you would find the turret a comfortable place in which to stay."

She knew he was being sarcastic, but she had asked for it.

"I mean, do you want me to leave Easton Hall?"

"No, not unless you want to do so. Jonathan seems fond of you."

"And I of him."

"Then stay, but coax him out of these ideas of his; they do him no good."

She nodded and followed him down the stairs. As he raised the lantern, Harriet caught a quick glimpse of another

74

door, lying back along a narrow passage. He saw her swift glance, pausing to study the flicker of suspicion on her face.

"A store room, also empty. Do you want to look?"

She shook her head, the momentary doubt gone, and in another minute they were back in the corridor and Easton was locking the door behind them.

They went down the back stairs together, and when they reached the ground floor they found a commotion which drove the thought of the turret out of Harriet's head.

Mrs. Tate was there, with Comper, Rawlston and Mrs. Grace, standing in a circle about a thin child of sixteen or so whom Harriet recognised as Agnes, the girl who came from the village twice a week to help with the scrubbing.

Agnes was crying, and Mrs. Tate and the cook were trying to soothe her when Valentine said impatiently:

"What is it? Be quiet, girl!"

Agnes stopped at once, overawed by Easton, the other servants bobbing their heads to him in quick respect.

"Comper? What's this all about?"

Comper cleared his throat.

"It is really nothing, sir, nothing at all. This foolish girl has come with another of those wild stories."

"What wild stories?"

Comper's tongue moistened his lips, as if his mouth had grown parched.

"About the hearse."

"For God's sake!"

Valentine's face was thunderous but, even in his anger, Harriet thought suddenly and quite inconsequentially, that he was the most attractive man she had ever seen.

"It's true." Agnes's face was wet with tears. "I ain't makin'

75

it up. It's true. It was seen again last night, large as life."

"Hardly an appropriate simile," said Easton briefly, and gave Agnes another frown. "Did you see this . . . this . . . thing?"

"No, sir, no, not me. If I'd 'ave seen it, I'd 'ave died on the spot. No, it were me uncle. Come 'ome late, 'e did. Not often 'e does that nowadays: no one in the village does for they know what they might see. But 'e couldn't 'elp it last night, and as 'e crossed Widders Walk, it turned into Church Road.

"Did he follow it?"

Agnes looked at her master as if he were mad.

"Oh, no! No one would follow the 'earse. It would be death, for sure. No, 'e ran in the opposite direction."

"Am I missing anything?"

Harriet turned quickly as Michael Paris descended the stairs with casual unconcern.

"I heard some disturbance, and hoped that it might be something which would divert me."

He exchanged a long look with Valentine, and Harriet was again aware of the taut communication between the two men which needed no words to aid it.

"I'm afraid you are doomed to disappointment," said Easton finally, and dismissed the servants with a brief wave of his hand. "It is only the phantom hearse again."

Paris took the thin cigar out of his mouth and smiled at Harriet. "Do you believe in ghosts, Miss March?"

"No." She was blunt, because she did not want Paris or Easton to think her a fool, yet Agnes's story had shaken her. Superstitious though the villagers might be, they must have seen something which had started the tale of the

76

hearse: something which was still seen every now and then. "No, Mr. Paris, I don't. Do you?"

The smile deepened fractionally, the hazel eyes still fixed on hers.

"Not usually, but I am beginning to wonder about this place."

Harriet made her excuses and started up the stairs again. She did not imagine for one second that Paris believed in spectres, but perhaps he had hoped to make her believe in them. She paused for a moment, hearing Easton murmur something. Then Paris spoke in a tone she had not heard him use before.

"Better she believes in ghosts than what is really happening, Valentine. Remember that, before you dismiss the hearse too lightly."

Three days later, Harriet and Jonathan met Kate in the village. Jonathan was better, and Easton had agreed that a breath of air would do him no harm. He seemed quite carefree as they left the Hall, humming to himself as he trotted down Lords Walk by Harriet's side, holding his face up to the weak sun which was trying to break through the clouds.

He and Kate took to each other at once, and he was quite content to sit with them for a while on a bench at the side of the Green. After a time he wandered over the grass, kicking a stone in front of him, and Harriet said:

"I'm sorry I haven't been able to see you again until now, Kate, but Jonathan has been ill and upset." She filled in some of the details of what had happened at the Hall, and then went on to the séance at Lantern House. "Miss Batsby was in a trance." She paused, a faint doubt assailing her.

77

"At least, I think she was. It wasn't her voice we heard, unless she was disguising it.

"I think it's dreadful, Miss Harriet," said Kate unhappily. "You shouldn't have gone. You're a Christian girl, and what they're doin' is wrong."

"Perhaps. It seems harmless enough, although some strange things did happen. I don't mean the flowers and the guitar, because I suppose those could have been faked somehow, but there were other things which I didn't understand."

"I don't like any of it. I wish you wouldn't go again."

"I must." Harriet was firm. "There is more that I want to know, and I have the feeling I might learn something at Mrs. Drewhurst's. Kate."

"Mm?"

"Do you think Eliza drowned in Calder Mere?"

Kate turned her head.

"No, Miss Harriet, I don't. She were born 'ere. She wouldn't go near Calder Mere. Everyone knows 'ow deep it is, and there've been drownings enough there to warn us off. Besides, Calder Mere is a long way off. Why should Eliza go there?"

"I don't know, unless someone took her there. But I didn't believe it either. Have the people in the village heard what Miss Batsby said?"

"Oh, yes, it soon got round." Kate grimaced. "Not much misses them. They think it's true enough but, like you said, that Eliza was taken there."

"By whom?"

Kate looked down at her hands.

"By Fred Humble, of course. Did you hear about Rosie

Forest?"

"I heard the servants at the Hall say something. A man in her room, wasn't it?"

"So she says. Samuel Forest is that cut up about it. He's asked everyone; offended some of 'em, I shouldn't wonder."

"Has he found the man?"

"No, and now everyone says it was. . . ."

"Fred Humble."

Harriet fell silent, watching Jonathan playing with his stone. Since Fred Humble was an impossibility, someone else had to be responsible for the going of Eliza and Ada, and someone else had to have entered Rosie Forest's room a few nights before, if the girl were telling the truth. It could be a local farmhand, of course. That would be a comfortable thing to believe, for it was uncomplicated and did not make her hands tremble as the alternative did. But most of the farmhands and labourers were married; their wives would have known if they had been missing.

She had to drag out the other possibility and consider it again, much as it distressed her. Paris had said some inexplicable things to Easton, and Easton himself was as free as the wind to go where he liked at any hour. Jonathan had seen someone on the landing who had run away when he realised that he had been seen. It made no kind of sense. Why should Easton run away from his own nephew?

She was glad when Jonathan returned and she could stop thinking about it. They made their way to the shops, where Harriet purchased cotton, needles and some toffee for Jonathan, and Kate bought a bag of flour and scraps of meat for the family's evening meal.

As they came out of the shop, Harriet saw the strangers

and paused. One was a tall, smartly-dressed man in a frock coat of worsted, with narrow whipcord trousers. He had a shiny top-hat and a neatly-trimmed beard. The other was fatter, and though his clothes were of good quality he did not seem entirely at ease in them.

"Who are they, Kate?"

Harriet nodded in the direction of the newcomers, and Kate frowned.

"The tall one's Alfred Prewitt; the other a man called Melrose. They're Londoners. They come for the seeances."

Harriet stared at them in blank amazement.

"Those two? Kate, are you sure. They don't look as if they would be interested in such things."

"I'm sure. They've been comin' off and on for the last six months or more. Ought to know better, the pair of 'em."

Harriet's astonishment had not abated. She had been told that people did come from London to Imogen's séances, but she had expected them to be gullible females, not well-tailored men who looked as though they belonged in city offices. She wondered what they hoped to gain from Imogen's trances and whether, whatever it was, was worth their journeys to and from the capital.

They were talking to Dr. Sawyer and it struck her that it was peculiar that they should know him, but then she shrugged. Why not? If they were regular visitors, they would soon get to know everyone in a place as small as Easton Mallet. As they drew nearer, she could see Sawyer's face and recognised the fear on it. Then commonsense made her shrug that off too. Men who drank heavily were not always in control of themselves; it meant nothing.

"I will try to see you in a day or two, Kate." Harriet

paused outside the forge. "Take care of yourself."

"I will, Miss Harriet, but it is you I'm worried about. You should never 'ave come 'ere and got mixed up in all this. You didn't 'ave to, you know, and...."

"I wanted to. When I got your letter, there was nothing else I could do."

"I shouldn't 'ave written."

"Indeed you should." Harriet patted Kate's arm and called to Jonathan who had run ahead of them. "Good-bye, Kate, and don't worry."

Half-way up the drive leading to the Hall, Jonathan took Harriet's hand. She looked down with a smile which faded when she saw his expression.

"Jonathan! What is it?"

"Did you hear what that man said, Miss March?"

"Which man?"

"The one from London."

"No, I wasn't near enough. What did he say?"

Jonathan's hand clenched tightly on hers as his voice dropped to a whisper.

"He said it to Dr. Sawyer, and Dr. Sawyer shook his head hard. He looked as if he were going to cry."

"But what did the man say?" Harriet was almost impatient. "What did you hear?"

Jonathan gulped.

"He said he was afraid that there was soon going to be another death in the village. Oh, Miss March, I don't like that man; he frightens me."

The next morning, very early before it was really light, Tom Crabbe and James Moffat were making their way

81

across the fields to Helsketh's Farm. They did not talk much, being men of few words, but theirs was a companionable silence as they trudged on in their thick boots and heavy twill smocks, their mid-day meal of chitterlings and a bit of bread and dripping in their pockets.

When they drew near to Parsons Pond, Tom said slowly: "See that, Jim?"

Jim looked up from the ground which he had been contemplating, screwing up his eyes as he followed the other's finger.

"Aye. By yon pond, you mean?"

"That's it. What be it, do you think?"

"Can't say from 'ere. Best get closer."

They moved towards the dark shape lying by the side of the water, hurrying now, faster and faster as they began to realise what it was that they were looking at. On their knees, they turned Samuel Forest's body over and stared at it open-mouthed.

Finally, Tom said dully:

"I reckon we'd better get 'elp, Jim. Samuel's dead."

When help came, including a sober Dr. Sawyer, Tom Crabbe's diagnosis was confirmed without doubt. Samuel Forest had been dead for some hours, so Sawyer said, drowned in the shallow pool into which he had fallen face downwards. His clothes smelt of spirits and those assembled looked at each other in surprise. It wasn't like Samuel to drink too much, nor to have the money to spare for whisky, but then he'd been put out by what had happened to his daughter, and maybe by a few rough words with some of those whom he'd questioned. It was clear enough what had happened. Upset and worried, he'd had a few too many at

82

the inn, and perhaps bought a nip in a bottle to see him home. Taking a weaving course towards his cottage, he had finally succumbed to the drink and fallen with his face in the water.

Dr. Sawyer's report was more officially worded, but it came to the same thing. Samuel Forest had died by accident. His sister was sent for from the next village, and moved into the cottage with Rosie, who had made a brave show of her grief to win the sympathy and approval of the village. She wished she had had a black dress to make the picture more convincing, but Aunt Ruby had tied a dark ribbon round her hair and lent her a black woollen shawl for the funeral. She almost chuckled to herself as she walked beside the rickety farm-cart carrying her father's body. Aunt Ruby was a soft old thing. She would be no trouble at all to manage, and it would be all too easy now to slip out at night to meet Joe Thomas.

She watched the body lowered into the ground, pretending to cry into her handkerchief, but it was then that the thought struck her. Her father wasn't given to drinking. A hard man, as rough with his words as he had been with his hands, and plenty of other faults besides, but he wasn't a drunkard, nor had he liked the stuff, as she'd heard him say plenty of times in the past.

He'd been angry when he had heard about the man in her room, but for once he had believed her. He'd been asking questions about it, too; lots of questions of lots of people. Rosie swallowed convulsively. What if one of those whom he'd questioned had actually been the man in her room that night, and what if the man realised that her father knew it?

She gave a small shiver, and Aunt Ruby patted her arm.

FIVE

The next séance at Lantern House was held three days after Samuel Forest's funeral. All those who had been at Harriet's first séance were there, together with Alfred Prewitt and Albert Melrose, to whom she was duly introduced. They seemed harmless enough, although curiously out of place in such a gathering, but they were very courteous to Harriet and to their hostess as they took their places at the table.

Harriet saw Prewitt glance at Margaret Lester, noting the gleam in his eyes as he considered her figure with lingering admiration, but then the lights were put out leaving a single candle as before.

At first there was silence, but soon Harriet heard soft organ music playing a haunting refrain, and despite herself she could feel a prick of nervousness. It was stupid to be fooled, she told herself sharply. She had not come here to be gulled by parlour tricks, but to try to get information, yet the atmosphere had been so cunningly created that she could feel herself being drawn into its web.

When she saw the hand in the centre of the table, she gave a start, clenching her teeth to stop an exclamation. It was a small hand, with slender fingers tapping lightly on the wood, the wrist tapering away into nothingness. Then it began to move about, appearing to touch first one person then another and finally twisting away into the darkness like a wraith.

Harriet was conscious that the candle was growing nearer to the table. She could not see whether anyone was carrying it, or whether it was moving of its own accord, but when it came to rest near Imogen Batsby, the medium got to her feet, her eyes half-closed. The others watched in dead silence, even when Imogen appeared to grow taller and taller until she was some foot higher than normal. Harriet could hear a gasp from her right, and then the candle was snuffed out.

"Be still," said Mrs. Drewhurst soothingly. "No one must speak. Remember, you could do a great deal of harm to Miss Batsby if you make any sound."

Obediently, the small group swallowed their emotions and waited. When the candle was lit again, they could see Miss Batsby was seated once more, apparently her usual size, but now her eyes were tightly shut and she was breathing in a deep, jerky manner.

The light had retreated to the far end of the room and when the voice came it was low and gruff.

"It be a bad place this." The words were loaded with tears. "A real bad place. I didn't drown meself, you know, not me. I wasn't one for the drink, and everyone knows it. It was 'e what did it to me. You all remember that, and watch out for 'im."

"Is that you, Samuel Forest?"

Mrs. Drewhurst sounded very calm to Harriet, but then she was probably used to the séances and to the extraordinary noises which came out of Imogen Batsby's thin body.

"Are you saying someone pushed you into Parsons Pond?"

"Aye, it wasn't me. 'E thinks because 'e's powerful that 'e can do what 'e likes. Always was proud, you see, and now 'e's mad as well. Watch out, all of yer. Watch out."

Mrs. Drewhurst asked another question, but Forest, or rather the sound of his voice, had gone.

Harriet was shaken. She had no doubt that most present would assume that Forest had referred to Fred Humble, but what Samuel had said could apply with equal force to someone else. Proud and powerful, and now mad. She could feel the palms of her hands grow moist against the mahogany, hoping that the session was at an end, but all at once there was a glow from the far side of the room, and she saw what appeared to be a child's face in the centre of the nimbus of light.

"Who is that?"

Before Bertha's question could be answered, one of the farmer's wives screamed aloud.

"It's William! It's my son, William! Oh mercy, what's 'appened to 'im?"

There was instant confusion, as chairs scraped on the floor and lights were called for. When the room sprang into view, Imogen was ashen, leaning over the table, gasping as if fighting for her breath. Mrs. Drewhurst was flushed and distinctly annoyed.

"Mrs. Potter, haven't I warned you all not to speak? Now, see what you've done. Taylor, take Miss Batsby into the morning-room and let her rest."

When Imogen had been led out and the tearful and apologetic Mrs. Potter calmed, the party broke up. Mrs. Drewhurst nodded to Harriet in a kindly fashion and more distantly to Lucy Morton.

"Mr. Prewitt, Mr. Melrose." She turned to the two men, inclining her head graciously. "Seeing that you've come so far for this occasion, may I not press you to a little sherry before you leave? If you will come this way. . . ."

She led them off to her small sitting-room near to the front door, whilst the others were shown out by Taylor. As the maid was about to close the front door, she heard Mrs. Drewhurst call out to her and turned quickly. The tone was sharp, and she knew better than to keep the mistress waiting when she was in one of those moods.

Margaret Lester had reached the gate before she realised that she had left her gloves behind. She swore mildly to herself and turned back. It really was getting to be rather a bore, coming to Lantern House, and Mrs. Drewhurst was unspeakably vulgar. There really didn't seem much point in coming again, for any entertainment value that there had been had long since gone, and she was tired of old Batsby's conjuring tricks.

She was surprised to find the front door open, but it saved bothering Taylor. The poor woman always looked so harassed, and no wonder. Anyone who had the misfortune to work for the Drewhurst was deserving of any consideration she could get.

Margaret collected her gloves from the parlour, looking round the room to see if she could discover how the apports had appeared or how the face and dancing hand had been engineered, but there was nothing to be seen. She shrugged. Well, it wasn't of any consequence.

She left the parlour and made for the front door, noticing

the light was on in the sitting-room on the other side of the hall. She smiled mirthlessly and looked over her shoulder. Taylor was nowhere about, and it was unlikely that Mrs. Drewhurst's other servants would come up to this part of the house at that time of day. It would be interesting to see what old Drewhurst was saying to the two men from London. Margaret had seen them both before, and had noted with scorn Prewitt's interest in her.

To her delight, the sitting-room door was also open a crack, just enough for her to see the solid outline of Mrs. Drewhurst as she sat in the velvet armchair, sipping her sherry. She put her ear to the crack, wondering what on earth such an unlikely trio could find to talk about, but after a moment she straightened up, the amused curiosity wiped from her face as she heard footsteps coming. She turned and fled, running down the path in the most undignified way until she reached the gate. She did not wait for her brougham, but began the journey back to Chase Manor on foot, thankful when the carriage came into view and she was able to get in and wrap the rug about her knees.

She thought about Valentine on the way home, her eyes half-closed with contentment. She hadn't expected him to stay the other night, after what had been said between them, but he had, and she had enjoyed every moment of it. He had been almost savage, as if he hated her, but she hadn't cared about that. She didn't like tame men, and no one could accuse Valentine Easton of being tame.

It was when she alighted from the brougham that she realised she had dropped one of her gloves again, cursing to herself, for they were expensive suede, newly-sent from France. But her annoyance did not last for long. No doubt

90

Taylor would find it on the path, where she, Margaret, had probably dropped it.

With that, Margaret forgot the whole incident as she went indoors and sat down to write another pointed note to Valentine.

When Harriet met Kate Plum the next day, Kate looked upset.

"Aren't you well, Kate?" she asked in quick concern. "You are so pale."

"I'm well enough, Miss Harriet. Shall we go inside?"

Kate took the kettle from the fire and began to make tea, Harriet sitting by the hearth and watching her. After a moment, she said:

"What is it, Kate?"

"It's everything, really." Kate let the tea draw, perching on the edge of her chair. "At first, when it was just Eliza, I was sad, of course, 'specially seeing that Ada had gone as well. I didn't think nothing of what was bein' said at first, at least, not too much. But things are gettin' worse now."

"Things?"

"Well, the man in Rosie Forest's room, and then her father bein' found dead. The 'earse was seen the other night, too, and only last evenin' there was lights seen in the chapel."

"How do you know?"

"Old Isaac Broom saw 'em, and 'e wouldn't lie." Kate sniffed. "Oh, Miss Harriet, I do reelly think there is something very wrong 'ere."

"So do I, Kate." Harriet was sober. "I'm not sure what it is, but I agree with you."

"Isn't is clear enough what it is?"

Harriet gave a wan smile and accepted her cup with a word of thanks.

"You can't blame everything on to poor old Fred, you know. There could be other reasons."

"But what, miss? Who else would do these things, and why?"

Harriet could feel the chill about her, wishing Kate's fire was larger, trying to pick her words carefully so that she might sound Kate out without committing herself too far.

"Well, it could be someone else in Easton Mallet. What about Dr. Sawyer, for instance?"

She said it almost jokingly, and Kate shook her head.

"No, not 'im. I daresay 'e ain't all 'e should be, but not 'im."

"Well, then, what about Mr. Long?"

"You're not serious? The rector? Why should 'e do such dreadful things?"

"I don't know, but he's afraid of something."

"Maybe, Miss Harriet, and so would I be, livin' where 'e does."

"Ah, Kate, but he should know better than to be afraid. He is a man of God. Phantoms shouldn't frighten him, but perhaps something else does."

"I don't understand."

"Never mind. Who else is there? What about Alastair Carrington?"

Kate shook her head.

"I doubt if 'e would 'ave the strength to do much, for all that 'e's a funny one."

"How funny?"

"Nervous, yet sometimes. . . ."

92

"Yes?"

"Sometimes 'e seems all excited somehow. Can't explain it proper, but it's as if 'e's worked up about somethin'."

"Mm. And what about the women?"

"It couldn't be a woman."

"Why not?"

"Well, the girls ... you know. ..."

"You may be wrong about why they disappeared." Harriet hesitated. "You think a man might have taken them for obvious reasons, but what if a woman was jealous of them?"

Kate stared at her blankly.

"Jealous of our Eliza? But why would anyone be jealous of 'er? Poor little mite, she didn't 'ave much in life. Barely enough food to eat and a few rags to wear. What's that to envy?"

"She was young, Kate, and pretty," said Harriet softly. "You said so yourself."

"Yes, but . . . oh! You're thinkin' of Miss Morton." Kate's mouth was unhappy. "Yes, I reckon she did hate Eliza, and Ada too, probably, but she couldn't 'ave done Samuel Forest in."

"Margaret Lester?"

"She's not one of us, miss. I don't know why she come 'ere, for it's clear she's no time for us."

"She came to be near to Sir Valentine," said Harriet in a small voice, avoiding Kate's eye. "We haven't talked about him, Kate, or Mr. Paris."

"No, we haven't, miss."

They sat and stared into the fire for a while, drinking another cup of tea, drawing some comfort from each other before Harriet said reluctantly:

93

"I'll have to go, Kate."

"Yes, Miss Harriet, Take care."

"I will."

They held each other's hands for a moment and then Harriet turned away quickly, whilst Kate sat down again to think about the expression on Miss Harriet's face when Valentine Easton's name had been mentioned.

That night Harriet heard voices again. She sat up in bed and flung the clothes back as she reached for her robe. This time they did not seem to be so loud, and when she went out of her room there was a brief silence. She peeped in on Jonathan, but he was sleeping soundly, and she breathed a sigh of relief as she went back to her room.

She waited, sitting on the side of the bed, thinking about Valentine Easton. When the voices began once more, it seemed to her that they came from outside. Quickly she crossed the room and moved the curtains aside the slightest bit, so that if anyone were below her window they would not notice her.

She saw the man on the horse directly below. He wore a black cloak and his head was uncovered, the wind stirring his dark hair. For a second he raised his head. His face was shadowed, but she caught the briefest glimpse of his profile before he drove in his heels and rode off.

She felt a hollow sickness in the pit of her stomach as she got into bed again, praying that when morning came there would be no tale of horror to tell, because now she knew that Valentine had ridden off at two a.m., perhaps to see Margaret Lester, perhaps not. Only time would tell.

At the same time as Harriet March had prepared herself

for bed, Margaret Lester went into her bedroom and closed the door, leaning against it for a moment as she looked about her. Usually, her room gave her a feeling of peace and tranquillity, but to-night something about it was different. She moved over to the dressing-table, considering her face in the mirror.

It was difficult to analyse the feeling which was disturbing her normal composure. She was not sure whether it was pique, because Valentine had not responded to her latest letter, or another emotion which she did not want to contemplate too closely. The red lips tightened. She had never been afraid in her life, and she was not going to start now.

She undressed slowly, swallowing up time by leisurely movements. She knew it would be difficult to sleep, and she did not want to read. All she really wanted was to be with Valentine, but Valentine wasn't there.

She was about to get into bed when she heard something which made her hand tighten fractionally on the sheet as her head turned quickly to the door. The house was empty; Horton was visiting her sister and would not be back until the morning. The other servants did not live in, for Margaret could not bear too many people about her. Besides, since she had come to Easton Mallet to be near Valentine, there was no point in discouraging his visits by cluttering the house with gossiping maids.

Then she relaxed. Perhaps it was Valentine himself, for he had a key to the front door, and although he hadn't used it as much as she had hoped he would, who else could it be at that time of night?

Margaret had many faults, and was the first to admit some of them, but timidness was not amongst their number. She went out into the passage and began to walk towards the top of the stairs. It was very dark, for all the gas-lights were out, and now her bedroom door had swung shut behind her, leaving her in total blackness.

For the first time in her life she felt something running down her spine which she recognised as fear, cursing herself for not bringing a lamp or candle with her. She hesitated half-way along the passage, straining her ears for a repetition of the noise. She had the oddest sensation, as if someone or something were behind her, but that was impossible. She would have known if there had been anyone close by; she would have heard them.

She pulled herself together with an effort. It must have been Valentine who had entered the house. A furious Valentine, because she had written to him again in such terms, determined to frighten her out of her wits to teach her a lesson. Well, he wouldn't do that, and she straightened her shoulders, her fingers holding tightly to the rail of the banisters, beyond which was the black void of the hall below.

"Valentine? Is that you?"

There was no reply; no sound at all. She tried again, placating now, since it was clear that he really meant business.

"Valentine, answer me; I know it's you. You're the only one who has a key. Why won't you speak to me?" She gave a small, artificial laugh which rang with hollow insincerity in her ears. "You're angry, aren't you? About my letter, I mean. I'm sorry, but you shouldn't have neglected me so. Valentine?"

She ventured another step or two and then stopped abruptly. The stillness was uncanny, and she could feel something on the back of her neck, just as if someone were behind her, breathing deeply. She twisted round with a half-smothered exclamation, reaching out a hand in front of her, expecting at any moment to encounter the solidness of a body beneath the smooth cloth of an evening cloak. But her fingers met nothing but empty space, and she moaned inside herself as she turned back.

"Valentine, listen to me! I know that you're there. I heard you. Why don't you speak to me? If you are cross about my note, let us talk about it. Come down to the sitting-room where we can have some light. I'll get you a whisky and we can discuss it sensibly."

Her voice was unnaturally loud, and now growing panic was making its edges ragged with a kind of anger of her own.

"Do you hear me? For God's sake say something. Don't be so childish. After all, I know what you've been doing, and I could. . . ."

She broke off again, putting her free hand to her mouth to stop the scream which welled up in her throat. The sound had been very soft, but she had heard it, and the rage drained out of her quickly, leaving her limp and uncertain.

"No! No, I did not mean that. I didn't mean to threaten you, but there seemed no other way. You had grown so cold, as if you couldn't bear to have me near to you. I had to make you see that I could not live without you."

She was shivering, conscious all at once that she had not stopped to pick up her robe, and that there was a strong draught blowing along the corridor.

Her hand found the newel post and she clung to it, feeling the clammy sweat between her shoulder-blades, knowing that she was in the grip of a terror such as she had never dreamed of.

If only it was not so dark. She couldn't see a thing in front of her, and her bare foot explored blindly the first stair. Again she paused. What if the sounds had not been on the bedroom floor? What if they had come from downstairs? She shrank back against the newel post, torn with doubts. Should she turn and attempt to reach her bedroom? At least the gas-lights were on there. Or should she get downstairs somehow and go for help?

But what help was there? Her heart sank dully, like a stone falling through the surface of a pool. There wasn't anyone from whom to seek help. She had chosen Chase Manor because it was so isolated; elected to have daily help because she wanted privacy. Even if she could get to the front door and run outside, what would be waiting for her? Not the warmth and relief of other human beings, but merely the tall trees and secretive shrubs which circled round the house and locked it away from prying eyes.

"Valentine!" She made one more effort. "Tear the letter up; destroy it. I didn't mean what I said. I will never speak of the matter to another living soul, nor will I say another word to you about it." She was almost crying now, begging him as she had never begged in her life, willing to do anything which would soften him so that he would mock her with that cool sardonic voice and turn the lights on. "I swear I mean it. Dearest, you know that I would never betray you, no matter what you had done. You know that, you must know that! Valentine...."

Then it came again. It was only a thread of sound, but to her sensitive and cringing ears it was like a clap of thunder.

She whimpered, feeling her heart pumping violently. She had no doubts now. There was someone there; she thought she could hear him breathing, but she wasn't sure, yet she knew that he was very close.

"Valentine. . . ."

She whirled round, her foot on the first step when she felt the heavy blow on her back. The recognition that she had been struck, and the awful sensation of falling through space, lasted only a fraction of a second.

By the time the tall figure in the corridor had lit a candle and walked unhurriedly downstairs, Margaret Lester was beyond hearing or seeing anything. The man paused for a second to consider her wide, sightless eyes and the dreadful angle of her neck. Then he blew out the candle, crossing the hall with quick, easy strides and closing the door softly behind him.

The news of Margaret Lester's death reached the Hall mid-way through the next morning. Harriet had left Jonathan in the library to wrestle with some simple French verbs, making her way to the kitchen to get a cup of tea. She found the servants gathered round the table, agog with the sensational tidings which the boy from the village had brought with the sacks of flour ordered by Mrs. Grace. For once, they did not seem to shut Harriet out, making room for her and handing her a thick white cup and saucer as they motioned her to sit down.

"You've heard, miss?" The cook's face had lost none of its normal colour and she was clearly excited. "Have you been told?"

"No." Harriet felt her heart lurch, and was glad to take

the chair because she was afraid her legs would not be able to bear the tidings which Mrs. Grace was so obviously determined to announce. "No, I've heard nothing. What has happened?"

"Why, the widow's dead, that's what." It was Heggarty who answered, pushing a strand of hair under her cap. "Found this morning by 'er maid when she got back from 'er sister's. Dead as a doornail."

Harriet forced herself to take a mouthful of the strong sweet tea, hoping it would steady both her voice and her hands.

"What happened? Was she taken ill?"

"Not likely." Pearce's dreamy look was not in evidence that morning, and her eyes were alert. "Lying at the bottom of the stairs with 'er neck broke, that's what."

"Oh, no!"

Harriet could not prevent the cry of protest, but the others did not seem to find anything extraordinary in her reaction. Indeed, it seemed to please them, for Mrs. Grace said soothingly:

"There, there, luv, no need to upset yerself. It were probably over quite quick "

Mrs. Tate nodded.

"That's so, she wouldn't have felt much. No need for you to trouble your head, miss, she was nothing to you."

"Ah, but she was something to someone in this 'ouse, wasn't she?" Heggarty was pert, smiling knowingly at Rawlston, who scowled back at her.

"None of that, if you please. It's none of your affair. You just attend to your business, and leave others to attend to theirs."

"I was only just saying," began Heggarty, aggrieved by the rebuke, "All I meant was. . . ."

"We all know what you meant." Comper was repressive. "Mind your p's and q's, my girl, or you'll find yourself in trouble."

For a second Harriet met Comper's eyes. She thought he looked pale, and that there was something behind his impassive mask which smacked of guilty knowledge. Then she looked away, hardly hearing the others as they returned to the topic of the widow and her untimely end. She had seen Valentine ride off last night. Although she had not had a good look at him, the brief glimpse had been enough to tell her who it was. She had prayed all night that nothing would happen during the hours of darkness and when she had first arisen and found the household as normal as ever, she had almost wept with relief. But now Margaret Lester was dead, and Valentine Easton had not been in his bed when it happened.

She said slowly:

"Was it an accident?"

They turned to stare at her until she felt her cheeks begin to burn.

"An accident?" Mrs. Tate said it as if the word were bitter on her tongue. "Of course it were. What else could it have been?"

Harriet almost shrank under the curtness of the housekeeper's tone, but then Heggarty sniggered.

"She means was it Fred, Mrs. Tate."

Mrs. Tate's mouth was a thin line.

"Of course it weren't, don't be absurd. And you, miss." She looked back at Harriet. "Put those ideas out of your

101

mind at once. They're nothing but a pack of lies, and you should know better, an educated woman like you. It was an unfortunate accident, as Dr. Sawyer says. Mrs. Lester must have got up to get a drink of water or something and didn't take a candle with her. Missed her footing in the dark, and that's all there is to it. Now, miss, if there is nothing else you want. . . ."

Harriet had outstayed her welcome, and she got up quickly, not sure how she managed to get to the door and up to the hall. She desperately wanted to believe Dr. Sawyer and Mrs. Tate's plausible explanation, but somehow it was difficult. If nothing else had gone before, it might have been easier to do, but as it was the suspicion burrowed deep into her mind and refused to be dislodged.

She stopped suddenly, hearing voices in the morning-room, not sure how to pass the open door without being seen flattening herself against the wall, feeling like a criminal.

Paris said sharply:

"For Christ's sake, Valentine, do you think I don't know what happened to her?"

"You have no proof."

"I don't need proof; I know. Who else would be responsible for this but. . . ."

"You are too quick to accuse, my dear Michael. It could have been an accident. That is what Sawyer says."

"Sawyer is a drunken fool, and this was no accident. No one knows that better than you."

"She was a blackmailing bitch." Easton's voice was like a rasp, and Harriet winced at the undiluted venom in it. "She is no loss."

"She was in love with you."

"She was in love with no one but herself."

"This can't go on much longer." Suddenly Paris's voice was flat, quite unlike his normal, half-amused tone. "You know that."

Harriet waited for no more. At the risk of being spotted she fled across the hall and almost fell into the library, biting her lip hard to stop her teeth chattering and summoning up every ounce of her self-control to meet Jonathan's surprised blue eyes.

SIX

It was sheer desperation which drove Harriet to leave the Hall that night. The death of Margaret Lester and the conversation between Easton and Paris had shaken her badly, and although her suspicions were hardening into a pain which she could hardly bear, she was still no nearer to solving the riddle of Eliza's disappearance, nor was there any proof against Valentine.

She had not liked Margaret Lester, but the thought of her lying at the foot of the stairs with a broken neck was appalling. Dully, she accepted that Easton was probably responsible. If Margaret had been blackmailing him, it was a situation which he would not have tolerated for long, yet what had that entirely personal matter got to do with the hearse and the lights in the chapel?

Since there was no obvious answer she must try to find one, and the chapel seemed as good a place to start as anywhere, for it was at the heart of the puzzle which was terrifying Kate and the others in the village.

She left the Hall by the side door which was kept unlocked at night. She had discovered that quite by chance, assuming it was the way in which Valentine came and went on his nocturnal wanderings, but now it was useful to her too. The walk down the drive was not a good beginning.

The moon was up, and so she could find her way easily enough, yet there were mysterious noises in the bushes and sudden darting movements in the undergrowth which made her heart leap into her mouth.

When she finally reached the gates she stood outside them, looking across the darkness in the direction of the churchyard, her resolution almost melting away. It was such a long way to go, over empty meadows and twisting cart-tracks. What if she were to meet someone . . . something? What could she do, out there in the open?

She forced herself to be rational. Who would be out there at that time of night? None of the villagers, certainly, and she had already assured herself most firmly that she did not believe in ghosts. And if she was afraid to try to solve the riddle, why had she come to Easton Mallet in the first place?

She didn't remember much of her journey, for her mind was too full of her unhappy thoughts, and it seemed to her that it was almost no time at all before she was standing by the lych-gate, hesitating as she peered into the sullen church-yard beyond. She had hated it by day, and it was no less terrifying by night, yet she had not come so far to turn back now, and somehow she forced herself to open the gate and go inside.

The churchyard seemed larger in the dark. The moon was fitful here, for there were so many trees making skeletal canopies overhead, and so many headstones to avoid that a circuitous route was inevitable.

At one point she paused, certain that someone was follow-ing her, but there was no movement behind her and so she moved on.

Eventually she came to a clearing from whence she could

105

see the outline of the chapel. She would have to go inside, even if the building looked like a sinister hulk, crouched down waiting for its prey. It wouldn't be pleasant; she knew that. It would smell of death, and drip with cold, stale water, yet it had to be done.

She had taken the first steps down the beaten path when she saw the blur of light from one of the arched windows. Her mouth drained of saliva, and she screamed silently to herself that it was sheer imagination. That it was a trick of the moonlight which made the glow bob about, but then she closed her eyes in fearful resignation. It wasn't imagination or the moonlight. There was someone inside the chapel; someone with a lantern, moving about.

The wash of terror which flooded over her was so intense that for a moment she thought she was going to faint, but then she managed to overcome the initial panic as her frantic mind fought off thoughts of Fred Humble. He didn't exist, so it had to be Valentine Easton, but what was he doing here at one o'clock in the morning?

The wind was rising, sighing through the trees and suddenly Harriet's battered determination deserted her. She turned and ran, as she had run once before, stumbling over tangled grass and weeds, splashing through stagnant puddles until she reached the gate. She did not look back as she made her way across the fields. Whatever was in the chapel, she did not want to see it now. All she wanted was the safety of her own room, with the door locked securely behind her.

It seemed hours to her before she reached the Hall, her breath tearing at her throat, her hair straggling down her shoulders where spiteful twigs had loosened the pins. When she finally got to her room and saw herself in the mirror she almost cried aloud. She looked like a phantom herself, white of face, with eyes which were not pleasant to see.

She would have given anything for a hot cup of tea, but the thought of leaving her room again that night was not to be countenanced, and so she undressed quickly and huddled under the bedclothes, leaving a candle burning to give her some small measure of comfort.

As she closed her eyes she could feel the tears on her cheeks, knowing that they were not entirely the result of fear, or a knowledge of her own faint-heartedness, but something much deeper and more painful, which she was still not prepared to drag into the open and face honestly.

Finally, when she was too tired to think any more, she fell asleep and dreamed of Valentine Easton.

Later that week, Rosie Forest slipped out of Glebe Cottage. Aunt Ruby was very easy to handle, quite a different proposition from Samuel, and Rosie smiled to herself as she heard Ruby's snores vibrating gently as she passed her room.

This was not the first time that she had crept out at night to meet Joe Thomas, and it wouldn't be the last. They had discovered a small, disused hut in Church Field, not far from the pond in which Rosie's father had been found dead, and they met there two or three times a week. Rosie was untroubled by the proximity of the pond, for she had already dismissed her father from her mind. She had forgotten about the man in her room too, for there had been no further sign of him, and now all her thoughts were for Joe and the happy hour or two which they would spend together.

She turned south, walking along Church Road until she

reached the narrow track which led off into the field, humming lightly to herself, her smile wide as she saw Joe running up from Widders Walk to meet her.

Inside the hut it was dark and dusty, but Joe had brought a candle and matches with him, and there was nothing wrong with the floor for what they had in mind.

Joe watched her, admiring the plump firmness of her young body, feeling himself growing warm with anticipation.

"Did anyone see you, Rosie?"

She giggled.

"Who's there to see?"

"Your aunt."

"Not 'er. She was snorin'. Nothin' wakes 'er."

"Easier than when yer father was alive."

Rosie tossed her head. She didn't want to be reminded of Samuel Forest now.

"Oh, him!" She was undoing the bodice of her frock. "He's gone, and I'm glad of it."

Joe nodded silently. He also was glad that Forest wasn't around any longer, for he'd always been scared that the tough, horny hand of Rosie's father might have descended on him too, yet there was something rather cold-blooded about Rosie's attitude. Then he shrugged to himself. Couldn't blame her, really, seeing what sort of time she'd had with her pa.

They came together like young animals, wild and eager and without shame. Sometimes, when their love-making was done, Joe would worry a bit in case a baby came, but whilst he was holding Rosie in his arms and could feel the warmth of her against him, he quite forgot the risks involved.

Afterwards, they lay together on the floor, not caring

108

about the dirt or the icy draughts, laughing together and teasing each other. The candle was burning down, but in any event its light was scarcely strong enough to reach the tiny window on one side of the hut. It was only a patch of glass, so dirty as to be almost useless, and neither Rosie nor Joe ever gave it a second glance.

They weren't looking at it now, and so they did not catch the blur of a white face with a lock of hair falling over the brow. All that they were conscious of was the feel of each other's hands and the contentment of the aftermath of love.

But soon even Rosie began to feel chilly and they got to their feet, brushing their clothes.

"Day after to-morrow?" Joe fastened his bootlaces and grinned at her. "Are you game?"

"Of course." Rosie had tied her hair back and was pulling on her shawl. "I'm as game as you, Joe Thomas, and don't you think otherwise."

They kissed outside the hut, holding hands for a long minute before Joe turned away and went off whistling into the night. Rosie watched him go; then with a deep satisfied sigh, began to walk back to Glebe Cottage.

At first she wasn't thinking of anything but Joe, and the wonderful, unbelievable feeling which the climax of their love-making brought to her body, making it vibrantly alive and tingling with something which she could not explain. She would never have dared to go so far whilst her father had lived, and she and Joe had had to make do with holding hands or the quick, furtive feel of Joe's fingers on the bodice of her dress. Now, it was different, for there was no one to interfere.

She came out of the thicket of trees on to Church Road

and then stopped. She could have sworn that she had heard something. Not the usual night sounds of the countryside, for she was used to them, but something else which was weird and unfamiliar. She wasn't too frightened at first, pursing her lips in puzzlement rather than anything else. She dismissed the matter with a shrug and started off again.

She could see the bulk of Easton Church some way ahead of her, not even remembering the chapel and the rumours which surrounded it, when she became aware of a peculiar rumbling noise, and of footsteps behind her.

She turned sharply, seeing a man not far behind her, faceless in the shadows. The rumble came closer, and Rosie began to run. Her lungs were bursting, and now she was terrified, every thought of Joe and their passion gone from her mind as she raced on. Suddenly her foot caught in a rut and she went sprawling, the wind knocked out of her, her chin striking the ground with a force which rendered her nearly senseless.

She was sobbing as she tried to rise, too stunned to do more than get to her knees, but when she looked up, every drop of blood drained from her face as she stared with blank horror at what was in front of her.

The noise in her head was deafening, like iron wheels grinding over hard stone, and her eyes were signalling messages to her brain which were totally unacceptable. She moaned and tried to get to her feet, but there was something on her shoulder, pressing her down with an irresistible force.

Her last conscious thought was that her father would never believe her when she told him what she had seen. He would say that it was just another excuse for being late, as he began to unfasten his belt.

Then the noise and fear and the sensation of being crushed were gone, as Rosie slipped quietly away from reality and into a bottomless void where nothing could ever touch her again.

Rosie Forest was found wandering in Potters Piece at about six o'clock on the following morning. It took the men who were on their way to Helsketh's Farm some time to realise that there was something wrong with her, for at first sight she seemed her usual self, except that her faded pink dress was slightly torn and rather dirty. For a moment or two the men joked with her, for Rosie was always a good sport and never took offence, but when she did not respond, they took a harder look at her.

Later, when Dr. Sawyer had had several cups of strong black coffee, he too had a look at Rosie and made his pronouncement. Briefly, and reduced to layman's terms, Rosie Forest's mind had gone, and she was just a pretty vegetable with a cloud of tangled gold hair and unpleasantly vacant eyes.

The barometer of fear in the village was badly shaken by the event, and the women huddled together as they met in the general store, whispering and speculating on what Rosie had seen which had turned her into a witless imbecile overnight. Joe Thomas was questioned, but he was too terrified to admit that he had been with Rosie on the previous evening, claiming loudly that he had not seen her for three days. No one really believed him, but, on the other hand, no one suspected that he had been responsible for what had happened. In the end, the villagers agreed unanimously that it must have been Fred Humble, or perhaps the girl had caught a glimpse of the hearse. Either would have been enough to turn anyone's brain, they said, shaking their heads. No wonder the poor child had gone mad.

Lucy Morton was in the linen-room at Lantern House when she heard the news. She was resentful because there was only a handful of embers in the grate, and the tea which the kitchen maid had just brought her was half-cold. She was making a new gown for Mrs. Drewhurst, rich Ottoman satin embroidered with flowers, and she smoothed the material between her fingers with a mixture of pleasure and envy.

When Mrs. Drewhurst brought Imogen Batsby in to show her how the dress was progressing, she mentioned the fate of Rosie, and Lucy looked up quickly, the needle pricking her finger and making her wince.

"But what did she see?"

"No one knows." Bertha's placid face was untroubled by the tragedy. "She doesn't say much, you see."

"But surely she has said something."

Lucy looked at Imogen, but Imogen wouldn't meet her eye.

"No, not really." Mrs. Drewhurst picked up a piece of the silk and admired it under the lamp which had had to be lit because the morning was so overcast. "Isn't this pretty, Miss Batsby? Such richness, don't you think?"

Imogen murmured something non-committal, but Bertha seemed satisfied, laying the material down again and reverting to the original topic.

"No, all the girl talks of is her father. She thinks he's still alive, but much of what she says doesn't make sense. In any event, she can tell us nothing of what happened last night."

"How dreadful." Lucy said it mechanically, reaching for a reel of thread. "What will happen to her?"

"Oh, she'll be all right with Ruby Forest." Bertha was unconcerned. "No need to worry about Rosie."

"What if she remembers one day?"

Lucy said it almost to herself, but the other two women turned their heads to look at her, for there was something in the tone of her voice which could not be ignored. The uncomfortable silence lasted for at least a minute, then Bertha said smoothly:

"No likelihood of that. The girl's mind has gone, so William Sawyer says, and he ought to know. Don't make the sleeves too tight, Miss Morton. You skimped the material on the yellow foulard, you know, and it's never really been comfortable."

Percival Long listened to his housekeeper's account of the affair, and his face grew a shade greyer. The corrosive feeling of guilt was eating him away inside, but he dared not let Mrs. Wallace see it, for it would be all over the village in a trice. He drank his weak tea and thought about the previous night. He had heard something, it was no good pretending that he hadn't, but he had not been able to bring himself to get out of bed to see what was going on. When he had pulled the curtains back at about midnight, he'd seen the lights and felt the old, familiar terror clutching at him like unseen hands. He should have gone to see what was in the chapel, then perhaps the girl would still be all right. Instead, he'd drawn the curtains again and pulled the blankets over his head, ignoring the lights and the sounds which he had heard later as he had tried to court sleep.

"I'll go and see her to-day," he said to his housekeeper,

113

who was waiting expectantly for such a promise. "Poor child, poor child, what a terrible thing to have happened."

By mid-day, William Sawyer had drunk three-quarters of a bottle of spirits. He had seen Rosie Forest and had done what he could for her, which wasn't much, but the sight of the girl had driven him home in a hurry to seek the only kind of solace which helped. He took another gulp, feeling the whisky burn his throat, wishing that he had never heard of Easton Mallet or any of the people who lived there. Some were harmless enough, of course, but others were not. Perhaps he could get away; after all, what was there to stop him? Then his face turned paler as his shaking hand clenched on the glass. No, he wouldn't be able to go; it was no use pretending he could. He closed his eyes and let the whisky do its work, hoping that when he slept he wouldn't dream of Rosie's terrible blue eyes.

Alastair Carrington went for a walk in the woods when he heard the news, because he didn't want anyone to see his face whilst he thought about what had happened. It was better not to take any chances, and the woods were a good place to be alone. If he stayed with people, they might guess that he'd followed Rosie last night, keeping well out of sight as she made her way to the hut, and that after a while he had crept nearer and peered through the window. He had cursed that window because it was so dirty, but he'd been able to see enough, feeling giddy as he lurched away, waiting for Rosie to leave. He had seen the boy, whoever he was, going off in the opposite direction, whistling in his triumph. Then he'd come out from the bushes again and started after Rosie.

He hadn't been sure what he was going to do when he

114

caught up with her. He was furious with her for what she had done with that boy in the hut, yet he had been prepared to let her pay for her mistakes, and then forgive her.

Alastair paused, shivering violently as he tried to pick up the recollection of the previous night, almost crying to himself when he found his memory was clouding and he could not recall what had happened next. All he could bring to mind was the sight of Rosie ahead of him, the quickening of his own steps, and a feeling that he had reached out to touch her. After that there was a blankness. And now it was too late. He wouldn't be able to see Rosie again, at least, not by herself. Now, she would always be with her aunt, led about like an infant which could not fend for itself. Alastair sank slowly to his knees on the damp grass and dissolved into tears.

"The girl probably saw a shadow and imagined someone was after her."

Valentine said it crisply, brooking no argument.

The Hall was usually the last place to hear any news, but by lunch-time even Easton himself had heard of Rosie Forest's fate, and had called the servants together to put an end to their hushed whispers. Harriet, coming down the stairs, paused to listen to him, wondering why he was making such a point of silencing his staff.

Heggarty was crying, and Easton said tersely:

"Be quiet, girl, no one's going to hurt you. Mrs. Tate, can't you do something with her?"

Mrs. Tate's face was very set, but she snapped out an order and the unfortunate Heggarty lapsed into silence.

"I want to hear no more of this," concluded Valentine firmly. "It is most unfortunate, and sad that the girl should

115

. . . well . . . sad that she was so frightened, but it is over now. Get about your business, all of you, and don't waste the rest of the day talking about it."

When the servants had gone, Harriet came down to the hall and Easton turned to her quickly.

"Has Jonathan heard about this?"

Harriet nodded. "I'm afraid so. It's difficult to keep things from him when the servants. . . ."

Valentine's face was grim. "Do the best you can for him. Don't let him brood about it, or he'll be having more bad dreams."

"You do not really think it was just a shadow, do you?" Harriet knew she was risking another outburst, but she had to ask. She had to see his reaction, no matter how frightening the result. "It was something more than that, wasn't it?"

The irritation in his voice was gone and his face was expressionless as he looked down at her.

"My dear Miss March, how should I know? Perhaps it was the girl's imagination, perhaps not. I regret that I can't satisfy your curiosity but, of course, I wasn't there."

Their eyes met, locked together for what seemed to Harriet an eternity. Then she said quietly:

"No, of course not, I just thought. . . ."

"I advise against thinking of that kind, and prying too in matters which don't concern you. Whatever happened to the girl, we shall never know now, for she can't tell us and certainly no one else will do so."

He walked off without another word, leaving Harriet staring after him.

It was three days later that Mrs. Drewhurst invited Harriet

to tea. Harriet had not particularly wanted to go, but since she still needed information about all who lived in Easton Mallet, she considered it foolish to miss the chance of asking Bertha a few questions.

Tea was served in the small sitting-room, a light airy place with flowered wallpaper and a pale blue carpet.

"Well, my dear, and how are you enjoying life at the Hall?"

Mrs. Drewhurst handed Harriet a cup of finest eggshell china, smiling and spruce in a spotted satin gown bunched up to great importance at her ample rear.

"I . . . I am fond of Jonathan."

Harriet was aware of the lameness of her reply, but Bertha seemed to find nothing unusual about it.

"Yes, he's a nice little boy. Pity he has to live in such a place."

"Easton Mallet?"

"No, the Hall. Have one of these sandwiches, Miss March, you'll find them delicious. No, I meant the Hall. It's not a place to bring a child up in."

"Well, I suppose it is rather isolated."

Mrs. Drewhurst grunted.

"No, it's not that, as I'm sure you know, but you're right to be loyal to your employer. I like loyalty in my own staff."

Harriet was not quite sure what to say, yet she sensed she was getting close to some confidence which might be of real value. Fortunately, Bertha required no answer and went on at once.

"No, it's not a good place for the boy, or for a young gel like you either."

"I don't think I quite understand."

117

"A bad atmosphere," said Bertha and took a sip of tea. "How could it be otherwise with him there."

"Him?"

Harriet's throat was growing dry. She had been right: Bertha was about to gossip, and she waited dutifully for her hostess to finish her mouthful of cucumber sandwich.

"Valentine Easton, of course. A most unsuitable man to have charge of a child, and as for that man, Paris, well. . . ."

"He . . . he seems pleasant enough." Harriet was willing Bertha to go on, hungry for any crumbs which were going. "Do you know him?"

"No." Mrs. Drewhurst sounded reluctant. "But I've seen him, of course, and I trust my own judgment."

There was a pause whilst Bertha refilled the cups, Harriet holding herself tense, waiting for more, but Bertha had done with Michael Paris and Easton too.

"You'd be better off here with me, my dear, as my companion. It's quite lonely sometimes for me. Of course, I've got Taylor and the other servants, but that's not the same thing. One can't talk to servants. But you and I would do well together, I think. What do you say?"

Harriet gaped. It was the last thing she had expected, but she did not want to offend Bertha, particularly as she hoped to attend future séances.

"Well, I hardly know what to say. I am grateful, of course." Harriet was quick to make this clear, wishing Bertha's eyes were not fixed so firmly on her face. "But I couldn't leave Jonathan."

"So loyal." Mrs. Drewhurst nodded benignly, but she was not yet done. "Have you finished your tea, dear, if so let me show you the room you would have. Such a pretty room for a gel like you; quite unlike that dark old Hall."

Harriet found herself led upstairs and into a bedroom decorated in pink and white. There were lawn ruffles on the bedspread and dainty silver and crystal fittings on the dressing table, with flowers in a bowl on the window cill.

"Now, isn't that charming?" Bertha smoothed the coverlet with a proprietary hand. "I'm sure there's nothing like this up at the Hall."

"No, there isn't, but. . . ."

"And you could have some new clothes too." Mrs. Drewhurst's penetrating gaze took in Harriet's neat but shabby brown dress with its modest trim of velvet and mock-silver buttons. "Come, look at these."

In the small room adjoining there were huge presses full of clothes of every colour and material. Harriet stared at them blankly, wondering what on earth Mrs. Drewhurst was doing with such a galaxy of gowns, all of which were clearly too small for her. Bertha saw the sudden doubt in Harriet and laughed.

"No, they're not mine. I'm afraid the days are long gone when I could get into those. No, they belonged to my niece, poor child." The smile had gone and Bertha was touching the corners of her eyes with her lace-edged handkerchief. "Such a lovely girl. It was such a shock when she died of pneumonia."

The handkerchief was whisked away again, and Bertha said brightly:

"You could have your pick, my dear, if you came here. Pity to let them hang in the cupboard unused. See, this green taffeta would suit you a treat, and this tawny velvet too. Why don't you try one on?"

Harriet shook her head quickly, not sure why she was so revolted by the idea, but Mrs. Drewhurst nodded understandingly.

"Well, another time perhaps. Now what about my suggestion? What do you think of it?"

"I would have to consider it." Harriet did not want to cut her ties with Bertha Drewhurst, and so prevarication was essential. "You understand that I could not simply walk out."

"No, no, of course not. I understand completely, but think about it. It isn't good for you to stay there, especially after all that has happened."

Harriet looked at Bertha quickly.

"All that has happened? What has that to do with the Hall?"

"Well, we don't really know, do we?" Bertha was closing the door and leading the way downstairs. "But there's been a good deal of talk. I shouldn't gossip, I know, but you're a sensible girl and will know how to keep a still tongue in your head. Well, there was plenty said about Sir Valentine and Mrs. Lester, but I'm sure you know that."

"Yes." Harriet didn't want to think about Valentine and Margaret Lester, even though Margaret was dead. "Yes, I had heard something"

"Well, I'm not narrow-minded, like some, yet it did seem to me . . . ah, well . . . the poor woman's gone now, hasn't she?"

They were back in the hall now, and Bertha was smiling in a way which made Harriet flinch. Her hostess was trying to say something to her without using words, but she, Harriet, was not sure what it was and she could not bring

herself to ask an outright question. Instead she said hastily:
"I must go. Thank you so much for inviting me. It was most kind of you."

"No, no, it was kind of you to come and keep me company. You must come again and soon. And don't forget to think about what I have said. You'd be much better off here with me than you are with . . . well . . . good-bye, my dear."

Harriet walked slowly back to Easton Hall wondering why Bertha Drewhurst wanted a companion. Bertha never appeared to be lonely, and was almost aggressively self-sufficient. Perhaps she was merely thinking of Harriet's welfare, convinced that no young woman was safe under Valentine Easton's roof. Harriet almost laughed aloud. Easton was hardly aware of her existence, except as a kind of servant employed to look after his unwanted nephew.

She must stop harbouring doubts about everyone. Mrs. Drewhurst had merely been kind and generous, even to the extent of offering her late niece's clothes. As she reached the gates of the drive, Harriet paused. She had not thought to ask when Bertha's niece had died, but it could not have been long ago, for all the gowns and cloaks had been of the latest fashion. There was something wrong with that, but she could not think what it was, and it was not until she was at the front door that the inconsistency struck her.

Bertha Drewhurst's beloved niece had just died, and she had wept for her, but in an age when death and its trappings were the all-consuming obsession of the conventional, Mrs. Drewhurst was not wearing mourning.

SEVEN

Mrs. Drewhurst's invitation, and some of her comments, kept Harriet awake that night. She had no intention of leaving the Hall, unless Valentine Easton dismissed her, but equally it was important to keep Bertha believing that the proposal was still being considered.

By now, Harriet had dismissed the lack of mourning wear as an insignificant detail: probably Mrs. Drewhurst hated wearing black, or perhaps she was not so conventional as some. Whatever the reason, it was not important.

Jonathan had been very silent that evening when she took him his milk and biscuits, as if he was thinking very deeply about something which he did not want to divulge to anyone. She respected his privacy, kissing him lightly on the brow as she tucked him up, grateful for the small smile he managed to give her when she lit his bed-side candle.

By two o'clock, Harriet was convinced that she would never sleep until she had some water to quench her thirst, but the carafe was empty, for she had forgotten to fill it earlier and, as Mrs. Tate had said in the beginning, the servants had something better to do than to wait on her.

She did not relish the idea of going downstairs in the dark to the kitchens, but the alternative was a wakeful and uncomfortable night, and so she put on her dressing-gown

122

and took a candle to light her way.

She stopped to look at the door of the west turret, just visible by the glimmer of a gas-lamp turned down low. What a fool she had been to imagine that there had been anyone there; she ought to have known better than to listen to a child's nightmares. Of course, the voices were still unexplained, but at least they had not come from the turret, and that was some relief.

She was half-way downstairs when she became conscious that there was someone on the staircase with her, coming towards her in the gloom. She felt her flesh creep, holding the candle up, praying the wavering gleam would not go out in the draught.

For half a second she thought she saw a familiar face, or rather, part of it; a dark curl of hair and the contour of a thin cheek. Then the candle went out. She caught her breath, waiting for Easton to speak, demanding to know what she was doing up at that hour. But nothing happened. There was neither the sound of a voice nor of footsteps retreating downstairs. Finally she forced herself to move, groping back to her room and re-lighting the candle. It needed a supreme effort to venture back again, but she had to be sure that there was no one there. She looked down at the empty landing, wondering if her mind were playing tricks on her.

She went back to the bedroom, shaken by uncertainty. She knew she would not be able to ask Easton about it in the morning. If she had been wrong in what she thought she had seen, he would think her mad. If she had been right, and he had been coming upstairs secretly, then it would be too dangerous to raise the subject. She lay back against her pillows, further away from sleep than ever.

123

If it had not been her overworked imagination, why had Easton been coming up to the second floor in the middle of the night, when there was no one there but she and Jonathan, a few empty rooms, and the deserted turret?

The next day there were no lessons, for it was Saturday. Harriet, looking rather peaky through lack of sleep, took Jonathan to the village where she met Kate Plum in the general store. Kate looked worn, too, and they hardly spoke until their purchases were completed and they came out into the dullness of the morning. They walked along Mill Road towards *The Sexton's Arms* with the intention of turning off just before the inn, where a narrow track led into Potters Piece. Harriet had bought Jonathan a new hoop at the store, and he was full of delight and anxious to try it out.

"There's Mr. Prewitt and Mr. Melrose," said Harriet suddenly, stopping short as she saw the two men in conversation with a third man whom she had not seen before. "Kate, who are they talking to?"

Kate shook her head.

"Don't know, Miss Harriet. Never seen 'im before."

"He looks like. . . ."

"Like what?"

"A sailor."

"What makes you say that?" Kate was puzzled. "How can you tell?"

"I can't be sure, of course. It's just the look of him. His skin is so brown, and did you see the way he moved just then? My father said that seamen walked with that rolling gait, because they were used to keeping their balance on board ship."

"I see."

Clearly, Kate thought the matter of no importance, and Harriet dismissed it too as they moved on to the grass and let Jonathan run off with his hoop.

"What is the latest news in the village, Kate?" Harriet folded her gloves carefully and tried not to see the unhappiness in her companion. "Is there anything new?"

"Nothing much." Kate was subdued. "There was Rosie Forest, of course."

"Yes, of course, poor Rosie. What do people think happened to her?"

"They're not sure. All they knows is that she saw something what frightened her 'alf to death. Perhaps it would 'ave been better if she 'ad died of fright, rather than live like she'll 'ave to from now on."

"Doesn't she say anything at all?" Harriet felt guilty at pressing the matter. It seemed so heartless in view of what had occurred, but it might be important. "Hasn't she said anything which helps?"

"Nothin'. She don't talk much, 'cept a word now and then about 'er pa, but that's all."

"Perhaps she saw someone."

"Fred Humble, more likely as not, or maybe the 'earse."

"Oh, Kate!"

"That's what we believe, Miss Harriet, however much you may laugh." Kate was roused to defend herself, flushing slightly. "After all, what else could it have been?"

"I didn't mean to laugh, Kate." Harriet was instantly apologetic. It's just that it's so. . . ."

"I know, but there's no other answer."

"What about Mrs. Lester?"

125

"The widow?" Kate's voice had a quaver in it. "Well, she fell downstairs, didn't she?"

"And it was an accident?"

"Maybe."

There was another silence, whilst Kate thought about Fred Humble, and Harriet about Valentine Easton.

"Are people more frightened now, Kate?"

"Yes, they are, miss." Kate's eyes met Harriet's with something like desperation in them. "It's getting worse and worse, that's why. First Ada, then Eliza. No one took much notice of them, for it's true enough that they could 'ave run off, though I'm sure our Eliza didn't. Then Samuel Forest, and Mrs. Lester, and now Rosie."

"Rosie isn't dead."

"She might as well be, but I reckon it was the same thing what done for 'er as for the others."

Harriet changed the subject, seeing the gauntness of Kate's face.

"I went to tea with Mrs. Drewhurst yesterday. She has asked me to be her companion."

Kate stared at Harriet.

"Her companion, miss? Why does she want a companion? She's got Taylor and the others, and she's never short of visitors, what with them seeances and all."

"I don't know. Perhaps she didn't want one really, but just felt sorry for me living at the Hall."

"You won't go, Miss Harriet." Kate's tone was suddenly urgent. "Whatever you do, don't go there."

"Why don't you like her, Kate? You've never really explained that."

Kate sighed, her moment of energy spent.

126

" 'Cos I don't know meself. I just don't trust 'er. Don't go there, Miss Harriet."

"I can't leave Jonathan, so there's no need to worry. She seems to think Sir Valentine and Mr. Paris are a wicked pair." Harriet said it lightly, waiting for Kate's reaction. "I believe she thinks they mean me some mischief."

"What do you think, Miss Harriet?"

Kate was sombre, as she watched Harriet trying to conceal her real feelings.

"Oh, I don't think they do." Harriet tried to laugh, but her effort was a dismal failure. "I don't think Sir Valentine is really aware of my existence, yet...."

"Yes?"

Harriet hesitated, wondering if it were right to burden the already-distraught Kate with the tale of the man on the stairs, or the fact that Valentine had been out of the house on the night when Margaret Lester had died. Then she knew definitely and beyond doubt that she could not speak of those things, even to Kate. She would not let herself dwell on the reasons for her reticence, but they could not be mentioned.

"Oh, it's nothing. It is simply that he is a cold man, keeping everyone at arm's length, even his nephew."

"But not Mr. Paris."

"No." Harriet frowned. "Why did you say that?"

"It's as if they had a secret, ain't it? Everyone thinks it's peculiar that a man like Mr. Paris should come 'ere to live. After all, what's the reason? Why did 'e leave London for a place like this?"

"Why did either of them do so?" Harriet pulled a face. They were getting uncomfortably near to the subject she

127

was trying to avoid. "I wish I knew how Jonathan's father died. Jonathan said his uncle won't tell him and . . . and he thinks he might have been murdered. Oh, Kate, do you think he could have been?"

Kate shook her head slowly.

"Don't know, miss, I'm sure. Not here, at any event. Never lived round these parts; always in London. By the way, there is somethin' else I forgot to tell you."

"Yes?" Harriet was eager, grateful for anything. "What, Kate?"

"You know that young Mr. Carrington?"

"Yes, what of him?"

"Well, when 'e first come 'ere, we was told it was 'cos 'e 'ad been ill. No one said what was wrong with 'im, but folk thought it might be 'is chest or summat like that, seeing 'e's a bit frail."

"And now?"

"Dr. Sawyer let somethin' slip the other day when 'e 'ad been drinkin'. 'Is 'ousekeeper told Mrs. Wallace, and she told. . . ."

"Yes, yes, but what did he say?"

"That it weren't 'is body what had been sick, but 'is mind."

"Kate! Are you sure?"

"That's what 'e said."

"But if he were drunk. . . ."

"More likely to 'ear the truth then than at any other time."

Harriet watched Jonathan bowling the red hoop towards her, a new line of thought holding her absorbed. If Alastair Carrington were mentally unstable, and if he had been sent away by his relatives to some quiet spot where he could no longer bother them, was that the answer to what had been happening? Had he had anything to do with Ada's and Eliza's disappearance, and Rosie Forest's present condition? She clung to the possibility like a drowning man to a raft until Jonathan came up to her, his face alight.

"Isn't it splendid, Miss March? Did you see it spin along?"

"Yes, I did."

She said it absently, but she touched his cheek lightly with her hand to assure him of her affection.

"Watch again, Miss March. Look . . . watch me. . . ."

He was whirling off once more, running with carefree abandon over the rough grass, tapping the bumping hoop now and then with a small yellow stick.

But if Alastair had been responsible for something happening to the three girls, and if by some remote chance he had had a hand in Margaret Lester's death, he had not been the man on the stairs nor could he have been capable of conjuring up Fred Humble and the hearse.

She dismissed Carrington sadly. Weak in the head he might be, but he was not strong enough or clever enough to engineer the cloud of fear which hung over Easton Mallet.

"There's to be another séance soon," said Harriet after a pause. "I shall go."

"I wish you wouldn't." Kate's hands were clenched together, as if willing Harriet to abandon the idea. "It's dangerous, Miss Harriet, and wrong."

"There's no danger at all." Harriet smiled, this time with some humour. "Much of it is mumbo-jumbo, although I must admit it is neatly done. I'm not quite sure how Miss Batsby manages to. . . ."

"To what?"

"The voices." Harriet's amusement had faded. "Some of the voices which come in the dark aren't a bit like hers. How could she fake the deep tones of a man at one moment, and then speak like a small child the next?"

"I'm sure I don't know," said Kate hastily, "but I can tell you somethin'. It's the work of the Devil, that's what it is."

"She looks ill and worried."

"I'm not surprised." Kate was roused to indignation. "She deserves to be, playin' with things she don't understand."

"And those two men, Prewitt and Melrose. They don't seem the type to be interested in such things. Have they been to Easton Mallet often?"

"Quite a bit in the last few months, and folks is odd. You can never tell what they're like by appearances. Well, I've got to be goin'. You'll be all right?"

"Don't be silly." Harriet leaned forward and kissed Kate on the cheek. "Stop worrying about me, you goose. I'm quite well able to take care of myself."

They went their separate ways, but as Harriet and Jonathan passed by the inn. Prewitt and Melrose were still there, but now they were talking to William Sawyer, and even from some distance away Harriet could see the fear on his face as he mopped his brow and shuffled his feet on the cobbled path.

At eight o'clock that night, Alastair Carrington was packing a small valise. Louisa, the maid, had the night off, and Henry, the odd-job man, had gone to the inn for a tankard of beer. Alastair had been glad to see them go, for he wanted to make his preparations without interruption.

It was clear that he could no longer stay at Vine Cottage.

People had started to look at him in a peculiar way, nudging one another with a furtive elbow as he passed by. They were beginning to suspect him, and he dared not wait until those suspicions had hardened into something else.

He did not pack a great deal. Just some night things, his brushes, and a photograph of his mother, in a silver frame.

As soon as he had gone, people would say he had been responsible for what had happened to Rosie, and perhaps to Ada and Eliza Dodds as well. Maybe he had been to blame; he really couldn't remember. He had spent so many hours dreaming of them and what he wanted to do to them when he had summoned up enough courage to get them on their own, that perhaps the reality had occurred without him knowing it.

He took off the velvet smoking jacket and reached for his coat. He was about to put it on when he caught sight of something round a button on one sleeve. His mouth opened but no sound came, and his eyes were blank with despair as he loosened the threads and held them up to the light. Human hair, as pale and fine as gold gossamer. Rosie's hair. He whimpered and flung the strand away from him, closing the case with a snap and pulling on his coat. He had no idea where he was going, but that did not matter. The great thing was to get away from the village before it was too late: before people began to ask questions about him and then come in search of him to demand answers. He need not go too far off; perhaps to the next hamlet. There were too many things to hold him to Easton Mallet to leave it altogether, too much left undone. He slipped out of the house, shutting the door quietly behind him.

"I always said there was something funny about that young man." Mrs. Tate poured Harriet a cup of tea, addressing herself to Mrs. Grace and Comper. "Never did like him. Something sly there, I always thought."

"Alastair Carrington?" Harriet could not stop herself, although normally she knew better than to push herself forward into the others' conversation. "What has happened to him?"

"You might well ask." Mrs. Tate was not annoyed for once. "He's gone."

"Gone where?"

"No one knows. Just up and left last evening, while Henry had gone to *The Sexton's Arms* for a drop of ale."

"But perhaps he went out for a walk and was taken ill. Has anyone been to look for him?"

Comper looked at Harriet pityingly, as if he thought her a fool.

"He'd taken his case, miss. He's gone right enough, and there's plenty in the village at this moment who are asking why."

"Well, why do you think he went?"

"Can't be sure, miss, but maybe he'd been fooling with Rosie Forest."

"And Ada and Eliza, too," said Pearce hopefully. Could be 'e's killed 'imself in remorse? Or maybe he ain't gone far if 'e's plannin' on doin' summat else. After all, there's other young 'uns 'ere 'e might fancy."

"Be quiet, girl," said Mrs. Tate angrily. "Such a thing to say, and in front of the governess, too."

They stared at Harriet and once more she was the unwelcome stranger in their midst. She murmured her thanks for

132

the tea and left them to their speculation, encountering Michael Paris as she made for the stairs. It flashed briefly into her mind that it was unusual to find him in that part of the house, but then he said with gentle irony:

"I see that you have to fetch your own tea, Miss March. You are ill-used. I should complain to Valentine if I were you."

"It is no trouble, and I doubt if Sir Valentine would want to be bothered with such matters."

"It's time he did something about his staff. They've had too much freedom whilst he was in London, of course."

"Perhaps Sir Valentine does not intend to stay here long enough to make it worth while." She gave Paris an innocent look. "He may be growing tired of the country."

"Maybe." Paris slid a cigar case out of his pocket, his eyes not leaving hers. "On the other hand, he may settle down in time."

"It is not a restful place."

"The Hall or the village?"

"Both." She decided to be bold, since Paris showed no signs of wanting to let her pass. "Don't you find the house noisy at night?"

Paris lit his cigar with care, contemplating the end of it with reflective eyes.

"Not particularly, but then I sleep soundly. A clear conscience, you know."

"The voices do not trouble you?"

Michael's gaze moved from the cigar back to her face, his mouth moving in a faint, derisive smile.

"Voices, Miss March? Do you hear voices at night? How extraordinary. Have you been reading about Joan of Arc?"

133

She seethed inwardly. His mockery was infuriating, but then it did sound rather melodramatic to talk of voices in the night to a man who clearly had nerves of steel and no fear of the dark.

"No, I haven't, and you are fortunate to sleep so well, Mr. Paris, for you miss most of the disturbances, such as the man who rode off in the middle of the night, and. . . ."

"What!"

Paris's voice made Harriet flinch. He wasn't laughing at her now: he wasn't laughing at anything.

"What man?"

Harriet said coldly: "If you stayed awake you might see him too. Please excuse me, I must go upstairs."

At first she thought he wasn't going to move. Then he stepped aside, but as she passed him, his free hand reached out and caught her wrist.

"You do not look to me like a young woman who would take easily to being given advice, but nevertheless I shall risk that. Don't stay here. Go back to London."

"Run away, like Jonathan's last governess?"

It was she who was flippant now, glad to see the anger in him.

"If you want to put it that way, yes. In any event, go."

"Oh, I don't think so, Mr. Paris. London would be so dull after Easton Mallet, wouldn't it? After all, isn't that why you don't leave yourself?"

When she got to her room she drank her cold tea, marvelling at her own nerve. Paris's face had scared her as she had hurried upstairs, and she doubted that she had been wise to cross swords with him, but at least he had not got the better of her on that occasion.

When she went in to Jonathan's room, she found him curled up on the window seat, looking forlorn.

"Shall I read to you?" She sat beside him, considering the pallor of his face. Up to that morning he had appeared better, but now the shadows were back under his eyes and he seemed to have withdrawn from her again. "Would you like that?"

"No, thank you," he replied politely. "I want to think."

"What about?"

"Lots of things."

"Sometimes it is not good to think too much, especially about. . . ."

"Yes?"

He was still very courteous.

"Well, about unhappy things. Often it is better to talk to someone about them."

"I know." He was like a grave old man, nodding his head sagely. "But sometimes one cannot speak of things which are very private, can one? They have to be worked out alone."

Harriet eyed him dubiously. He was far too self-contained, and she longed to shake him until he unburdened himself of whatever it was that was troubling him. She thought it might be the death of his father, and it was on the tip of her tongue to ask, when he said:

"Did you know Mr. Carrington had run away?"

"Yes, Mrs. Tate told me. That is, she said he had gone. It does not necessarily mean that he ran away."

"I expect he did, like Miss Bailey."

"Do you know why she went? I know you said she was frightened, but what precisely made her go?"

135

"She saw something." Jonathan turned his solemn face to hers. "She wouldn't tell me what. Of course, there was the hearse and the other things, but in the end it was something else which made her go."

"I saw Mr. Paris downstairs." It sounded rather an inane remark, but she wanted to draw Jonathan on the subject of his uncle's guest without alerting him to her real interest. "Have you known him long?"

"No, I hadn't seen him until I came here."

"He seems a good friend of Sir Valentine's."

"I suppose so. Like David and Jonathan, you mean?"

She hid her smile. "Well, perhaps not quite like that. Do you like him?"

"He's all right, I suppose. He teases a lot, but I don't think he really says what he means."

"Oh?"

Jonathan had turned to look out of the window again, and she studied the small serious profile doubtfully.

"Why do you say that?"

"Well, he doesn't smile with his eyes. Have you noticed that, Miss March? When he says things to make me laugh, I feel that he is doing it to hide something else."

Harriet took a deep breath. Jonathan was far too precocious for comfort, and she said quickly:

"I expect it's nothing really. Are you sure you wouldn't like us to read together?"

"Quite sure." The words were firm, but gave no offence. "I must finish what I am thinking about, you see, otherwise it may be too late. And I don't want it to be too late, Miss March, I really don't."

136

Imogen Batsby got back to Pond House at eight o'clock. Her visit to Miss Morton had been long and tiring, for the stupid woman could not seem to get the sleeves of her new dress to fit properly. She wished she had never purchased the material, or considered having it made up, for what use were new clothes now?

Only the lamp in the hall was alight, and Imogen's heart sank. She had forgotten that it was Lotty's afternoon off, and that the maid would not be back until ten.

She hurried round the house, lighting gasoliers and oil-lamps in every room, breathing a sigh of relief when she could see that there was nothing out of place and no sign of anything but Lotty's careful housekeeping.

It was too much of an effort to make herself a meal, and so she went into the parlour and put some more coal on the fire. There was to be another séance soon, and she would have to give some thought to that. She needed help, of course, to make them sufficiently eerie and mysterious to hold the attention of her audiences, but none of the sleight of hand or illusions would have been any good unless she, Imogen, had had the real gift. And she knew that she had it. She had no idea what happened when she went into a trance, and had to rely on others to tell her afterwards what had gone on, but since they were always so satisfied with the results, it was clear that her calling was a true one.

She lay back in her chair and closed her eyes. She had not intended to go to sleep, but soon she was dreaming about Mrs. Smith and her imbecile son. She woke with a start, convinced that a noise close by had aroused her.

Unsteadily she got to her feet. Was it James Smith again? Had he really got in this time? Had she forgotten to shut

137

the front door properly? Somehow she got out of the parlour and into the hall. No, the door was closed firmly enough; he couldn't have got in through there, and she knew that the windows were fastened, for she had checked those herself as soon as she had got home.

She forced herself to look into all the rooms, upstairs and down, the feeling that she was not alone in the house growing stronger every minute. She got back to the hall and waited, trembling, because she was quite certain now. There was someone there.

When she heard the slight sound behind her she spun round, watching the kitchen door begin to open. She felt every ounce of strength drain out of her body, yet from somewhere she found enough energy to scream, the shrieks cutting through the silence and shattering it into fragments.

"Lord a'mercy, Miss Imogen," said Lotty, her face as white as her flour-covered hands. "Whatever be wrong with you? Are you hurt?"

Imogen sagged against the newel post, her cries dying into gasps.

"You . . . you . . . were out. It can't be ten o'clock yet."

"No, I was early back. Looked in on you, but you was sleepin' like a babe, and so I thought I'd make a pie for our supper. Oh, Miss Imogen, what is it, then, what is it?"

But Imogen couldn't answer, for sobs were racking her body and tears blinding her eyes.

"There, there," said Lotty finally, when Imogen was quiet at last. "What you want is a nice cup of tea. You be goin' back to the parlour, and I'll bring you one. A fine scare you gave me, I can tell you. Why, I thought at first you'd seen a ghost."

EIGHT

Jonathan Easton left the Hall at twelve o'clock precisely. He had never been out of bed so late before, and even though he had his small oil-lamp with him, the shadows were fearful as he crept down to the side door and let himself out into the cold, misty night.

It had taken him a long time to reach the decision to go. As he had told Miss March, it had needed a lot of thinking about, and it was something about which he could not talk to anyone else. For nights he had lain awake and considered the matter; by day the torment was always with him. In the end, the truth was inescapable. He, Jonathan Easton, was a coward.

He began his journey across the fields, his teeth chattering, tempted more than once to turn tail and flee back to the comparative warmth of his bed, but he forced himself to go on. Having recognised his weakness, the next thing to do was to defeat it, and he had had no difficulty in selecting the task to prove his valour. If he could get to the church and back, that would do. He could never accuse himself in future of being craven, scared of the slightest thing so that Miss March had to comfort him like a baby. Once he'd achieved his target, he could look her in the face again.

As he trudged on, his hands and feet grew nipped with

the chill air, and the mist blinded him one moment, sweeping aside the next to give his lantern the chance to reveal sinister shapes ahead.

He got to Farm Road, half-way to Easton Church, standing still for a moment to get his breath. At first, he could hear nothing but the whine of the wind in the trees, but then his quick ear caught another sound and his heart gave a sudden lurch. The rumbling noise grew nearer, but Jonathan could not move. He wanted to scream or to run until his lungs burst, but his feet were rooted to the spot as the thing came closer and closer out of the darkness until it was nearly on top of him.

He stared at it vacantly, almost too numb for fear. He had heard about it many times, of course, but now that it was here he could hardly accept the evidence of his own eyes.

There were two black horses, sable-plumed, and a fine hearse with a line of elaborate silver-work round the top. Through the glass-panelled sides he could just see the outline of a coffin, heavy oak with brass handles. The light he held picked up a chaplet of roses lying on top of the coffin, the sheen of the coach-lamps rubbed up like gold, and a black velvet pall, turned half-way back.

Jonathan's dazed eyes moved from the finely-turned wheels, larger behind than in front, upwards to the coachman's seat. Then the terror in him sprang to life again and the merciful numbness was gone.

There was someone sitting in the seat, clothed in black with a top hat and long crepe streamers. Jonathan raised the lamp, although one part of himself fought against looking at the face because he was afraid of what he would see.

Then the coachman bent down, and for a brief moment man and boy stared at each other in silence.

When the driver held out his hand, Jonathan gave one piercing cry as he turned and ran. He did not know how he got over the fields again. He had dropped his lamp in his terror, and now the mist was closing in to try to prevent him from reaching home. Yet in spite of his fear, the agony of his breath in his throat, and his near blindness, he managed to get to the side door, falling through it with a sob of gratitude.

He didn't know whether the hearse had followed him, but at least it couldn't get up the stairs to where he slept. He pulled off his clothes, freezing as he hugged himself into a small ball under the blankets.

He had failed. He had not reached the church, and when he had seen the hearse, which everyone knew was not real, all his firm resolutions had melted away. Under the bed-clothes he shuddered. The hearse might not have been real, but the man in the coachman's seat was. He had been flesh and blood and there could be no mistake about who he was either. Jonathan buried his head in the pillow. If only it had not been him. If it had been anyone else, it would not have mattered so much, but him. . . .

When Harriet went into Jonathan's room the next morning to take him down to breakfast, she was aghast at his appearance.

"Jonathan! Dearest, what is it?"

He shook his head mutely, keeping it bowed.

"You must tell me. What is it? Was it another dream?"

Again the negative motion of his head, and Harriet felt despair in her heart. He was shutting himself away from her

141

again, determined not to give her access to his private torment.

She sat on the edge of the bed, saying nothing until he was forced to look up. She almost wept at the haunted eyes, but this was no time for tears.

"Sit here next to me."

At first she thought he would ignore her, but after a moment he came slowly towards her, perching uneasily on the bed.

"I used to tell my father things," she said after a pause. "Not at once, because, like you, I felt some things were not right for sharing, but in the end when they became too bad, I used to tell him."

"Did you?" He was doubtful. "Did it help?"

"Oh, yes, enormously. My father was very wise, and a good listener. I'm a good listener, too."

He looked down at his hands again.

"Yes, I know, but if I tell you, you will be cross, for I did something I ought not to have done."

"We all do that sometimes."

"But this was really wicked."

Harriet felt a lump in her throat. He was so small and defenceless and so much in need of love and reassurance that she was mortally afraid she might fail him.

"I can't imagine you being really wicked."

"But I was." He met her compassionate gaze. "Last night I went out. I'm not allowed to do that, you know."

She felt a tremor run through her, but her voice remained calm and untroubled.

"You went out? Why, Jonathan? Why did you do that?"

"You wouldn't understand."

142

"I might. At least give me a chance to try."

"I had to prove that I wasn't afraid." Now that he'd got the first words out, the rest tumbled off his tongue in a rush. "I am not a baby now, yet I am always being frightened by things. I was sure that you'd think me a coward, and so I thought that if I went as far as Easton Church and back, that would prove that I wasn't, and then I wouldn't have to be ashamed any more."

She was crying inside, but she did not let him see it.

"That was terribly brave, but you did not have to do it for me. I never thought you a coward."

"But I didn't get to the church."

"No?"

"No." His voice dropped to a whisper. "I only got half-way, because . . . because . . . I. . . ."

"Yes?" She was brisk and practical. "Because it was so cold, I expect. It was very sensible of you to have turned back."

"It wasn't that. Not the cold, I mean. I saw . . . I . . . saw it, you see."

Harriet tensed. "Saw what, sweet?"

"The hearse." Jonathan was watching her reaction, thankful that there was no anger in her. It would be all right to tell her about the hearse now, but whatever happened he must not mention the man. If it had been a stranger, it wouldn't have mattered, but it hadn't been a stranger. "Yes, the hearse. I saw it. It was all black, and there were two horses and. . . ."

"Darling, are you sure?" Harriet's hand was over his now. "If it was dark. . . ."

"I took a lamp with me, and I'm sure. I saw the hearse."

"But. . . ."

"I did, Miss March, I did, I did!"

She soothed him at once, seeing the pent-up emotion rising in him, brushing his hair back from his forehead and kissing him lightly.

"We'd better go down," she said, and took his hand. "They'll wonder what has happened to us."

As they reached the small dining-room where they had their meals, Jonathan said loudly, as if determined to establish the point:

"I did see it, Miss March. I really did see the hearse."

When Valentine Easton sent for her, Harriet felt a small twinge of alarm. She had a strong suspicion that Jonathan had not told her everything, yet he was far too upset to be pressed at the moment. If Jonathan had really left the house the night before, and she was inclined to believe that he had, perhaps Valentine Easton had discovered the fact.

She found him in the study, sitting very still behind the desk, his face as unreadable as ever.

"You wanted me, Sir Valentine?"

The bright blue eyes moved slowly over her until she could feel embarrassed colour burn in her cheeks. Then he said:

"What's all this nonsense about Jonathan seeing a hearse?"

She gaped at him, totally unprepared for his question.

"H . . . hearse?"

"Yes, Miss March, hearse."

"But I don't understand . . . I . . . ."

"You understand perfectly well. You are not half-witted."

144

"But how did you know?"

"I heard what Jonathan said to you as you went in to breakfast. Now stop wasting my time. What did he mean?"

She stiffened at his tone, her moment of shock over.

"Perhaps you should ask him."

"I'm asking you."

"I cannot tell you very much, I'm afraid. You know as much as I do."

"I doubt that." His mouth was a straight line. "The boy talks to you. Did he go out of the house last night, or was he dreaming?"

He watched her face, distracted for a second by the perfection of the small, narrow nose, the curve of her cheekbone and the remarkable quality of her eyes. Then he shook off the irrelevance of his thoughts and repeated his question more sharply.

"I really have no idea." She lied boldly, determined not to let Jonathan's secrets slip from her. "I think it was probably a dream, don't you? Is it likely that he would really go out on a cold November night?"

"I don't know. That is why I am asking you." He sat up abruptly. "Miss March, if you are withholding facts which I should know. . . ."

"I'm not." She said it very rapidly, praying that her guilty face would not give her away. "I can assure you that I am not. Jonathan is a delicate boy and things upset him easily. He heard the servants talking about the hearse, and I expect it was on his mind when he went to sleep."

"I hope so." Easton relaxed again, but he still held her eyes with his own. "I hope that it was not more than that. If I find that you have not been telling me the truth. . . ."

145

"Yes?"

She did not back down, calling his bluff.

"My course of action would be quite clear." He refused battle, and stood up. "That is all, Miss March, thank you."

He watched her go. Even the drab grey dress she wore could not conceal the miraculous way in which Nature had fashioned her body, nor mar the grace with which she walked. He had always been very conscious of beauty and of beautiful women, no matter their station in life. He had thought Rosie Forest as lovely as Margaret Lester: one simple and fresh, the other polished to an exquisite perfection, but both desirable. And now Jonathan's governess, shabby and of no importance, but possessed of a loveliness which made his pulse quicken whenever he saw her. Yet she had been lying, of that he was certain, and if Jonathan had gone out of the house last night, and if he had seen something besides the hearse, then he was a threat.

The cold, handsome face grew very still again. If the boy had begun to understand the truth, then something would have to be done about it, and quickly.

Imogen Batsby took her place at Mrs. Drewhurst's table and looked round at those assembled for the séance. Some were missing, of course, for Margaret Lester was dead, and Alastair Carrington had gone. The governess from the Hall was there, looking rather white, and so were Alfred Prewitt and Albert Melrose, as well as Lucy Morton and the ever-faithful farmers' wives.

Imogen was conscious of a great sense of fatigue. The fright she had had the other night had not helped, and since then she had slept badly, starting awake every hour or so,

146

convinced that Smith was coming for her to take his revenge.

Mrs. Drewhurst had given her a glass of wine before she entered the parlour as she always did, and that gave Imogen a measure of false courage, and as the lights were dimmed, she felt the sensation of swimming, as if she were under water.

"She's off."

Mrs. Potter whispered it in Harriet's ear, and was rewarded with a reproachful hush from Mrs. Drewhurst, but then there was silence for a while, the candle providing only a glimpse of the group about the table.

There were no apports that evening: no flowers wet with dew, no twanging guitars. Harriet wondered dully what she was doing there, for what possible help could Imogen Batsby be to her? Yet she had not been able to stay away in case a single careless word from someone gave her a clue to what was going on in Easton Mallet.

She tried not to think about Valentine and his anger, nor about her growing certainty that he was at the heart of the sickness and terror which had struck the quiet little village. If Jonathan had been holding something back, was it the fact that he had seen someone as well as the hearse? If so, would he not have told her who that person was, unless it had been someone close to him, bound by blood-ties, whom he could not betray?

She waited for a voice to cut through the stillness. Clearly, Valentine was involved: everything which Michael Paris had said bore that fact out. They were hiding a secret, but what? She tried to prevent the answer rushing into her mind but was powerless to do so, shrinking as it thudded at her reason and forced her to believe. Valentine Easton might

147

have chosen to come back to the Hall, but Paris had had no
need to do so, unless he had come to watch Easton. To look
after him, and to control him, if he could.

"It wasn't an accident."

Harriet jerked to attention. It wasn't Imogen's voice, but
someone who spoke with a slow, husky drawl.

"That is Mrs. Lester?"

Mrs. Drewhurst never appeared to be in the least surprised when Imogen's throat produced the most unlikely
sounds. She asked the question as if she were enquiring the
time of day.

"Yes, it is I. You weren't fooled, were you? You did not
really think that I had fallen?"

"Dr. Sawyer said it was so, and we had no reason to dis-
believe him."

"He was wrong. I was pushed."

The faint gasp from the listeners was quickly stopped by
their hostess.

"That seems unlikely." Mrs. Drewhurst was unmoved by
the accusation. "Surely. . . ."

"Oh, yes, I was."

Harriet strained her eyes to see better, but the candle was
too far away. She wondered why Mrs. Drewhurst had taken
it upon herself to question the voices when they came, and
whether she had had previous experience of séances before
she had come to the village.

"There was nothing to show that it wasn't a mishap."

There was a low laugh.

"No, of course, there wouldn't be. He is too clever for
that."

"He? Who would that be, my dear?"

148

"Clever and cold and calculating, that's what he is. None of this would have happened but for him."

The shiver went round the table again. Everyone knew to whom Margaret Lester referred, and Harriet clenched her teeth to stop herself crying out in protest.

She forced herself to be sensible. It was all faked, every bit of it; it had to be. Imogen Batsby must be a mimic and a clever one at that, for every voice which Harriet had heard round the table had been easily recognisable. Margaret Lester was dead. She had been buried in the churchyard under a yew tree, and there was no possibility at all that she was now using Imogen to accuse Valentine. It was a clever, malicious trick, nothing more.

She sat frozen, her fingers still touching those of her neighbours, hardly hearing the rest of the questions, aware finally that the talking had stopped and the lights were on again.

It took Mrs. Drewhurst and Taylor longer that evening to rouse Imogen Batsby, and Harriet felt chilled as she realised that Imogen had been deeply unconscious. Could an unconscious person mimic another?

"Well," said Mrs. Drewhurst ten minutes later as she served hot coffee, "that's a fine thing, I must say."

"What . . . what happened?" Imogen's cup was rattling on its saucer in her unsteady hands. "What. . . ."

"Well, dear, it seems that Mrs. Lester did not think she fell down those stairs, but was pushed." The bright dark eyes were on Harriet's face. "Quite spooky, it was, didn't you think so, Miss March?"

Harriet took a sip of coffee, almost scalding her tongue. "Yes . . . yes, it was."

"It was Mrs. Lester?"

149

Mrs. Drewhurst nodded amiably at Imogen.

"Yes, my dear, it was. Quite upset too and no wonder if what she said were true, but that's something we shan't be able to prove, shall we?" She looked back at Harriet. "Come to tea with me on Sunday, Miss March. I think we ought to have another talk."

When Harriet went to Jonathan's room on the following morning and found he was not there, she was mildly surprised but no more than that. Usually he waited for her, and they went down to breakfast together, but perhaps he had been awake early and had gone out into the garden for a while. She glanced through the window, seeing the drabness of the day, frowning slightly. Well, perhaps he had gone to the library.

When she could not find him in the small dining-room, the library, or the garden, the nibbling alarm inside herself became a panic, and she called to Mrs. Tate and Comper to aid her in her search. Soon, all the servants were helping, and by the time Easton and Paris returned from their morning ride, the whole house had been thoroughly searched.

"But he can't have gone." Easton's face was disbelieving, his tone more so. "You can't have looked properly. Try again."

"But, sir. . . ." Comper was nervous but vehement in his denial. "We have looked properly. We've looked everywhere. The boy isn't in the house."

Harriet saw Valentine look at Paris and quailed. She knew Easton would make the servants search again, and knew equally that they wouldn't find Jonathan. She wondered what Easton had done with his nephew, and whether Jona-

150

than was already dead. So, he had seen his uncle on the night he had ventured out, and Easton had not been certain that the child would keep quiet about the fact.

"When did you last see him, Miss March?" Easton was brusque. "You were closest to him."

"I saw him last night when he went to bed. When I went to fetch him this morning his room was empty.

She wanted to shout at Valentine and demand that he stop pretending, but she couldn't. In any event, it was probably better not to challenge him at that moment, in case there was still some hope for Jonathan.

"This is ridiculous." Valentine said it roughly. "How can he have gone? Where would he go? Have the house searched again, and look more carefully this time."

The servants ran off hastily, for the master was in no mood for arguments, muttering to one another as they scattered through the house to try once more.

"What about the west turret?"

Easton's eyes were like ice.

"What about it, Miss March? The door is locked, and Jonathan has no key."

"I just thought. . . ."

"If it will put your mind at rest, I will look myself later, but I can assure you there is no possibility of him being there."

He turned away, and Michael said softly:

"Don't concern yourself; we'll find him."

"Will you, Mr. Paris?"

"Of course. He cannot have got far."

"Not on his own."

Michael's eyes narrowed.

"You think someone took him? But how? And who would want to do so?"

"I don't know." Harriet found it difficult to look at Paris. "I have no idea, but if he is not in the house, and I'm sure that he isn't, then where is he?"

"That is what we have to find out."

Paris nodded to her and moved past her, leaving her holding tightly to the banister.

She wanted to help the others to look for Jonathan, but she could not force her legs to move for the moment. All she could do was to remember that Jonathan had gone out at night, seen the hearse, and, if she were not mistaken, something or someone else as well.

She began to think about the hearse. Was it a phantom, as the villagers said, or was it a real one? If it was real, and Jonathan had actually seen it, what was it for? Why did a hearse appear every now and then and trundle through the outskirts of the village?

Half an hour later, even Valentine was satisfied that Jonathan wasn't in the Hall. He pulled on a heavy coat and said tersely:

"Some of you men look in the grounds. Mr. Paris and I will go further off and see if we can find him. Mrs. Tate, send someone to the village. Perhaps the boy has gone there, although why he should at this hour of the morning I cannot think."

By mid-day it was clear that Jonathan Easton was really missing. When Valentine and Paris came back two hours later they had no comfort to offer either.

"No one has seen him," said Easton. "We've been up to Calder Bottom, Shrewton and Basely. He couldn't have got much further than that."

"And Calder Mere?"

Easton turned his head to look at Harriet.

"No, he wasn't there either."

"You mean you didn't see him there."

"He had no reason to go there," snapped Easton. "For pity's sake, girl, use some sense. He knew the dangers of the mere as well as anyone else."

"Someone has taken him."

Harriet said it dully, not caring any more whether he raged at her or not. She was not even certain now whether Easton and Paris had been responsible for Jonathan's going. If they had been, would they have wasted so much time looking for him? Perhaps they would, if they had wanted to convince people that they had no knowledge of his whereabouts.

"It is just like Eliza and Ada Mullins."

"Nonsense! Those girls probably ran away."

"I don't believe they did."

"Perhaps you subscribe to the popular belief that that man Humble took them." He was biting. "Perhaps you think he's got Jonathan too."

"No, I don't." She wished her eyes were not filling with tears, for then she would have spat back at him. As it was, the words came out as a meek denial. "But someone else may have taken him."

"I hardly think so."

The anger was over and he was remote and untouchable again.

"Then what do you think has happened to him?"

"I think he's wandered off somewhere. We'll go out again in half an hour or so and try once more."

"What about the police?"

A definite reaction that time, and Harriet could feel the tension in him as if it were a solid, tangible thing.

"What about them?"

"They should be told."

"They could do no more than we will do. We have enough men to look for the boy. We'll get some men from the village to help later on."

"Were the police told about the two girls?"

"There are no police in Easton Mallet, Miss March." He was beginning to move away from her. "I doubt if anyone thought it worth travelling so far to inform them that two irresponsible serving wenches had run off."

That night, when Harriet went to fetch her tray, the servants were very quiet.

"Is there any news?"

Mrs. Tate shook her head.

"No, they've just come back, but they found nothing."

"What are they going to do?"

"I'm sure I don't know, miss. It's none of my business, nor yours neither. Sir Valentine will know what to do for the best."

"I reckon we shan't see Master Jonathan again." Heggarty had been crying. "He's gone the same way as them others."

"Hold your tongue." Comper was quick to silence Heggarty, but not too willing to look Harriet in the face. "Enough of that talk, if you please. What will Miss March think of you?"

Heggarty began to snivel again.

"I'm sorry, Mr. Comper, but it's that awful. That poor little soul taken off like that."

"Not taken off." Comper had a better grip on himself now. "He's run away, that's what he's done. Only a matter of time before he's found. Let me open the door for you, miss."

It was Harriet's dismissal, and she had no choice but to pick up her tray and leave the kitchen. Comper had been well-schooled, and she would learn nothing more from the staff that night.

It was very lonely on the second floor. She had not realised how comforting the thought of Jonathan next door had been, even though he was only ten years old. At least he was another living soul, but now she was alone with the dim gas-light and the long empty corridor. She wondered if Easton had troubled himself to go into the turret. Probably not, but it did not really matter because, as he had said, Jonathan hadn't got a key.

She ate her meal without tasting a mouthful of it, and then knelt by her bed to pray for Jonathan and his safe-keeping.

NINE

In the middle of the night Harriet woke with a start. She thought at first that she had been dreaming, but after a moment she could hear the voices, just as she and Jonathan had heard them before.

She looked out of the window first, but although it was a misty night, it was obvious there was no one there. Then she went out into the corridor, but as she did so the voices stopped abruptly. Gritting her teeth, she took a candle and walked the length of the passage to the turret door, but it was locked as usual. She turned and made her way downstairs, fearing that at any moment she would encounter someone, or that the sounds of anger would begin again.

When she got to the foot of the back stairs, she pushed open the door which led into the main hall, her hand cupped over the candle so that the flame did not betray her presence.

At first the silence was absolute, and she was about to turn away, almost convinced that it had been a dream after all, when she heard footsteps and saw the light of a lamp moving across the darkened hall.

". . . yet it cannot go on."

She had missed the first part of the sentence, but she recognised Paris's voice, and blew the candle out quickly.

"There is nothing I can do. I cannot help myself."

156

Valentine sounded weary, as if he were tired of arguing. "That isn't good enough." There was no trace of Michael's casual drawl now; he was clearly angry. "What you are doing is criminal, and if you cannot help yourself, then. . . ."

A door closed and they were gone.

Harriet let her breath go, shivering as she turned to grope her way upstairs again. So, Michael Paris did believe that Valentine was responsible, and even he was beginning to realise that he could no longer protect his friend.

When she reached the second floor she gave a muffled cry, the candlestick falling from her hand as she leaned against the wall. It was a trick of the light; it had to be. The gas-lamp was very low and the draught strong enough to make it flicker and create images and patterns which weren't really there.

Yet, if it weren't an optical illusion, the door of the west turret had just closed, slowly and without a sound. Harriet grabbed the candlestick and fled back to her room, locking the door firmly behind her.

"No news at all, Miss Harriet?"

Kate was hesitant to ask, seeing Harriet's set face, yet feeling some enquiry were called for.

"No, none." Harriet paid for the packet of pins and walked with Kate to the door of the shop. "They're out again now, but I don't think they will find him."

Outside, the wind struck them spitefully, whipping at their skirts and forcing them to cling to their hats.

"Maybe they will." Kate was comforting as she touched Harriet's arm. "Come and 'ave a cup of somethin' 'ot with me. You look all chilled up."

157

Over their tea, weak but piping hot, they talked again. Harriet would have liked to have blurted out all her fears and dreads, but that would not have been fair to Kate, and, in any event, something inside her made her hold back. She could not mention Valentine's name in the same breath as those fears. Not to Kate; not to anyone.

"What do people down here say?"

"In the village?" Kate put a few more pieces of coal on the fire, coaxing it into a small blaze with her bent poker. "Well, much what you might expect."

"The same as Eliza and Ada?"

"Aye. Them lights were seen again last night, too. Old Ebenezer Blye claimed 'e saw 'em on 'is way 'ome. Likely as not 'e did. Not one for makin' things up, is Ebenezer."

"Why doesn't someone go into the chapel to find out what it is?"

"No one would dare."

"By day, I mean."

"Oh, they've done that. Weren't nothin' to see. Lights only come at night."

"I wish they would let me help in the search."

"You can't do that, Miss Harriet; wouldn't be proper. Besides, what could you do that them strong men can't?"

"Nothing, I suppose, yet I feel so helpless. It is as though I don't care about him, but I do, Kate, I do!"

"I knows you do." Kate's hand closed over Harriet's. "Don't fret yerself, love. Maybe 'e did just wander off, like Sir Valentine says. If so, they'll find 'im in time."

"Will they? I wonder."

When Harriet left Kate's, she walked back to Pond House. Imogen Batsby answered the door herself, looking scared as if she had expected someone else.

"Forgive me." Harriet forced herself to smile, trying to drive the hunted look from Imogen's face. "I'm sorry to disturb you, but could we talk?"

"I suppose so."

Imogen seemed doubtful, but she led the way into the parlour and watched Harriet take the proffered chair. She had been in two minds as to whether or not to open the door, since Lotty was out shopping, but in the end she had risked it.

She perched on the edge of the sofa and said cautiously:
"What did you want to speak to me about, Miss March?"

"About Jonathan."

Imogen stared at her vaguely.

"Jonathan?"

"Yes, you must have heard that he is missing."

"Yes, yes, of course, but I. . . ."

"Can you help me to find him?"

Imogen's pale lips moved soundlessly, and Harriet sighed. What an idiot she had been to have come. How could she have brought herself to believe that the pallid, frightened woman sitting opposite to her could really do anything to help? Yet now she was here, she had to say something, although the faint spark of hope which she had nourished desperately on her way to Pond House was now totally extinguished.

"I mean, if you tried, could you tell us where he is? You were able to do so when people wanted to know where Eliza Dodds was."

Imogen flinched. She wanted to shout at the girl to go away and not to bother her. She was not a miracle-worker,

159

and how could she be expected to produce information like that to order?

"I don't know." In the end, she was polite and controlled, so that the governess should not see the rabid fear in her. "I don't know what happens, you see, when I go into a trance."

"But will you try?"

"I . . . I . . . I'll think about it."

"And you will let me know?"

"Yes . . . yes, I will let you know."

Harriet found herself outside Pond House with the door shut behind her. Imogen Batsby had been quivering with nerves, but perhaps that was not so extraordinary. Most of those who lived in Easton Mallet were frightened now. At first, they had managed to weather the storm, but now it was increasing in momentum, breaking over their heads in fury, and there were few to be seen as Harriet began the long walk back to the Hall.

She saw William Sawyer just about to open his front door, and stopped him, glad to find him near-sober for once.

"No," he said hastily. "I've no idea where the lad could have gone. Might be anywhere, the young scamp, but don't you worry your pretty head. The men will find him."

"But if they don't?"

"They will. Good-day, Miss March."

Further on, she encountered Percival Long, equally evasive.

"I will pray for him," he said after her first anxious questions. "Indeed, I have already done so."

She wanted to hit him for withdrawing from reality, but this was no time to lose control.

"I have just talked to Kate Plum. She says lights were seen in the chapel again last night. Did you see them too?"

His long nose was red with the cold, his eyes watering. He wished the girl would go away and stop bothering him. He'd already heard, but he certainly hadn't seen them, for he'd kept his curtains pulled well over the windows. The girl was looking at him accusingly, as if the lights were of his doing, and as if he had been responsible for her pupil's disappearance.

"No, no, of course not." He bluffed it out. "It's all talk, Miss March, nothing more. There aren't any lights in the chapel at night. How could there be? The place hasn't been used for years."

"Have you ever been in there?"

"Of course I have."

"At night?"

He hated her quietly. How dared she, an underpaid governess in a worn old coat and darned gloves, question him? She was a nobody; a servant.

"Yes, I have." The lie rolled smoothly off his tongue as he edged past her. "Yes, of course I have. There was nothing there. It's all silly talk, as I've told you. Good-day; I must be on my way."

When she reached the Hall, Valentine Easton called her into the study.

"We haven't found him." He said it bluntly, not attempting to soften the blow. "We've combed the woods on the far side of the church, but there was nothing."

"Did you look in the old mortuary chapel?"

He eyed her thoughtfully.

"I suppose you've been to the village. Were the lights seen

again? It's a favourite story they scare each other with, you know."

"Perhaps." She wasn't going to be put off. "But did you look there?"

"Yes, it was empty."

She might have believed him, if he had not lied about other things, but she let the matter go for the time being.

"What will you do now?"

"Go on looking. He may come back on his own, of course."

"Do you want me to stay?" She was submissive again, for she could not leave Easton Mallet whilst Jonathan was missing, and Kate's cottage was already desperately over-crowded. "May I stay here for the time being?"

"Of course." He seemed surprised that she should ask. "I am not as pessimistic as you, Miss March. I expect Jonathan to come back, and when he does he will need you."

He watched the relief flood into the amber eyes, wondering what she would look like in silk and diamonds. He was a fool to have employed a girl like this in the first place. She was too intelligent; too determined. Yet to send her away now, when she was already suspicious, would be an act of high folly. He would have to wait for a while before he got rid of her.

"Yes, of course you must stay."

"Thank you."

Harriet wondered what Valentine had been thinking about in that moment. His expression had been different; softer somehow, as if he had been considering something pleasant in the midst of ugliness. She had a sudden urge to touch his hand and to whisper to him that he could explain things to her if he wanted to do so: that she would understand, and would not judge him. Then the madness passed, and she left him, keeping her chin up and not letting him see the tears which had started to run down her cheeks.

"I'm so glad you came." Mrs. Drewhurst beamed at Harriet and put her head on one side. So pale, though, but that's not to be wondered at. Has he been found?"

"No." Harriet's tenuous hope for Jonathan's recovery was growing weaker by the hour. "They still keep looking, but there has been no sign of him."

"Nor will there be now." Bertha clicked her tongue. "Too long, you see. If he'd just wandered off somewhere, they'd have found him by now. As it is. . . ."

Harriet forced herself to be calm.

"But if he didn't wander off, what could have happened to him?" She refused to listen to the insistent voice in her head which told her that someone had taken Jonathan. She must ignore the deadly whisper, for she wanted to hear what Bertha had to say. "What else could have happened to him?"

Bertha shrugged, straightening her lace collar with a well-cared-for hand.

"Hard to say. If I were as silly as those villagers, I'd say Fred had taken him. As it is, well, I really don't know. Now, my dear, some more tea, and then we must discuss your future."

"My future?" Harriet was startled out of her dark thoughts. "I don't understand."

"Oh, haven't you remembered what we talked about last time you came to see me? I hoped you would have made up your mind by now."

Harriet flushed. She had completely forgotten Bertha's invitation to become her companion. So much else had happened, and she had not really taken the proposal seriously in any event.

"No, no, of course not, but Jonathan. . . ."

"Well, he's not there any more, is he?"

"But he might come back."

"And pigs might fly, as my mother used to say." Bertha was cruelly cheerful, apparently unaware that her words were like the cut of a knife. "No, dear, there's nothing to keep you at the Hall now, and if you're the sensible girl I think you are, you'll get out of there as fast as you can."

"I cannot simply walk out."

"Why not?" Mrs. Drewhurst helped herself to an iced cake and bit into it with relish. "What use will you be to Sir Valentine, now that his nephew's gone, pray?"

"I don't know, but. . . ."

"Well, there you are. Tell him you're leaving."

"Not yet."

Bertha looked at her over the rim of her cup.

"Not sweet on him, are you?"

Harriet winced. She had not realised before just how vulgar Bertha Drewhurst was, but perhaps that judgment was too harsh. Perhaps it was because of the pain the question brought in its wake which made her want to rush out of the room, away from the round pink face and black unwinking eyes.

"Of course not."

She told herself that she was not lying, and that that was why her denial had such a ring of truth about it. Bertha nodded.

"Just as well. You don't want to get mixed up with a man like that."

"I am not mixed up with him." Harriet was slightly haughty, warning Bertha to keep her distance. "He is my employer."

Mrs. Drewhurst laughed, not in the least put out by the snub.

"So he may be, but he's a handsome devil too, and you won't be the first to have been taken in by him."

"You mean Mrs. Lester?"

Harriet was still cool, and Bertha snorted.

"No, not her. She was as bad as he is. You know what they call women like her, don't you? They didn't even try to hide the fact that they were . . . well . . . you know."

"Then whom?"

"Oh, I'm not one to name names, but you get out of his house as quickly as you can. There's bad blood in his family."

"How do you know?" Harriet's curiosity and desperate need to know more about Valentine Easton forced her to come off her high horse and encourage Bertha to continue. "You know his family?"

"I know about some of them." Mrs. Drewhurst winked. "Bad lots, most of them."

"Did you . . . that is . . . did you know Jonathan's father?"

"No, I can't say I did." Bertha sounded regretful that her knowledge did not stretch that far. "The one who died, you mean?"

"Yes, Jonathan asked. . . ."

165

"What, my dear?"

Harriet hesitated, not sure why she had mentioned Valentine's brother at all, wishing Bertha was not hanging on her every word.

"Well, it's foolish, of course, but. . . ."

"Yes?"

"Jonathan did not know how his father had died. He wondered if he had been murdered."

Bertha nodded.

"I wouldn't be at all surprised. It is that kind of family. Now when can you move in?"

"Not yet." Harriet repeated it more firmly this time. "I am more than grateful to you, Mrs. Drewhurst, but I can't leave the Hall yet. I must wait a little longer, in case Jonathan does come back."

"Please yourself." Mrs. Drewhurst did not seem unduly put out. "I'm always here if you want me. Imogen tells me you've been to see her."

"Yes." Harriet was uncomfortable. "You'll think me a fool, but I just wondered. . . ."

"Why not?" Bertha was encouraging. "I'll arrange it for you. No reason why we shouldn't try. After all, Miss Batsby's had a number of successes: perhaps she'll have another for you. I'll let you know when."

When Taylor showed Harriet to the door, Alfred Prewitt and Albert Melrose were coming up the path. They raised their hats to Harriet politely, not looking back as Taylor ushered them inside.

Once again Harriet wondered about the two men, and how they could spare so much time from their business affairs to dally in Easton Mallet for Imogen's séances. Then

166

she shrugged them off. Perhaps they believed Imogen's voices would one day produce good advice about investments, and, in any event, as Kate had said, folks were queer.

When she presented herself in the study some two hours later to ask what the latest news was, she thought Easton looked worried and tired. He shook his head and Harriet gave a deep sigh of disappointment.

"I had hoped. . . ."

"And I."

"Is there anything I can do? Anything at all?"

"Not now. Not until he comes back, if he. . . ."

The missing words hung between them, forcing them into an uneasy silence. Then Easton said:

"Mrs. Tate says you have been to tea with Bertha Drew-hurst."

"Yes."

The blue eyes were reflective.

"I would not have thought that you had much in common with her, but then, of course, you've been to those damned séances, too, haven't you?"

She flushed, feeling a fool. No wonder he sounded so scornful. Would anyone with any sense attend them?

"They are . . . amusing. I don't believe there is any truth in spiritualism, but it passes the time."

"There are other and better ways to do so."

"Are you saying you object to my attending them?"

"No, what you do in your spare time is your own affair, providing it does not adversely affect Jon. . . ."

The silence fell again, heavier and more deadly than before.

"I don't believe in it; I really don't," said Harriet in a

small voice. "I wish you would accept that."

"I do." He gave a slight smile. "You are far too intelligent to be taken in by such trickery, and that is why I wonder what other reason you have for going to Bertha Drewhurst's."

"I've explained that. It passes the time."

"So you said."

"Is there anything more?"

He shook his head and she went upstairs, opening the door of Jonathan's room and feeling the moisture on her lashes again as she looked at the empty bed.

Then she walked over to the window, resting her hand on the wide sill. Jonathan kept a few china animals there, with a pile of books at one end. She picked up the top one, hardly seeing the title page, when a small sheet of paper fluttered out and settled on the carpet by her feet. She retrieved it, thinking it was merely a book-mark, but then she recognised Jonathan's childish scrawl. It was too dark in his room to read the note, and so she went back to her own and sat down by the lamp.

"I love you, Miss March," Jonathan had written. "Please don't go away and leave me."

Harriet folded the note up and put in into her pocket, her grief suddenly gone, for she knew now what she must do. She had been putting it off for too long, but Jonathan's secret and touching expression of devotion had roused her from her shameful fear and forced her to face what must be done.

If she thought Valentine Easton was responsible for what had happened to the child, and a good many other things besides, she must confront him with the fact. She could no longer avoid all the things which pointed to his guilt, pretending that she might have been mistaken, either because she was afraid of him, or because she was more fearful still of her feelings for him.

It would take courage, but that Jonathan had just given her. She would wait until after dinner, when the servants had finished their work and were down in the basement. Then she would find Valentine Easton and ask him just what he had done with his nephew.

TEN

When Harriet went in search of Valentine at ten o'clock there was no sign of him, or of Michael Paris. When she asked Comper where his master was, the man merely looked shifty and muttered something about a further search.

"But where?" She was impatient. "Have you no idea where they've gone?"

Comper looked startled at her tone, as if a small lap-dog had suddenly snarled at him.

"Well, I'm not sure, miss, but I thought I heard something about the churchyard."

Harriet watched him go and then made for the stairs. If Easton had taken his nephew, the chapel was the most likely place to hide the boy, for no one would venture there after dark. Its reputation had been too well advertised for that.

She had a sense of urgency now which made her run to the stables to find a horse. Walking across the fields would take too long, and she was thankful to find one of the stable boys still about. At first he objected, fearful of what his master would say, but she gave her orders in such peremptory tones that in the end he bowed to her insistence and saddled up the chestnut mare.

The ride across the fields seemed endless, but eventually she dismounted at the lych gate, tethered her mount, and went into the churchyard. It was just as dank and fearful as before, but now her desperate desire to find Jonathan made her ignore the soggy puddles and overhanging branches of trees which tried to catch her hair in their spiky fingers.

She saw the lights flickering in the chapel, holding back for half a minute to muster all her resources for the final push. Then she went forward and opened the door. The lamp swinging from the beam revealed the decaying stone walls and slabs, dripping with water and green with slimy moss. It seemed to be some kind of ante-room, for there was a second door ahead and gingerly she pushed that open too, holding her breath, half-expecting Easton to spring out and make an end of her.

She took a few tentative steps forward, still tense and very wary, not knowing what to expect but conscious that something was about to happen. Then she became aware of the girl lying on the ground and knelt quickly by her side.

The girl was a total stranger, with straight dark hair and a beautiful mouth. Her hands were tied behind her back, and she did not appear to be breathing. Harriet felt numb. The girl was not more than sixteen at the.most. Young, like Eliza and Ada, who had also vanished from their homes. She sat back on her heels, sick at heart. Why should Valentine Easton do this? Why did he have to take these children, for they were little more than that, to satisfy an obscene appetite?

She was wondering what to do about the girl when she heard loud voices outside and got hastily to her feet. It must be Valentine, yet it had not sounded like him, and there were others too. She crept to the door and opened it, giving herself a squint-hole to peer through.

171

It was too dark to see much, but the lamp inside the chapel gave her a quick glimpse of a tall, broad-shouldered man with black, curly hair. He half-turned, and she could see the faint outline of a high cheek-bone, and her last drop of hope faded. It was Valentine; there was no doubt of it. Before she could move, there were others. The backs of two men rushing at Valentine, and then a third, springing out of the night behind him. She wanted to scream, to warn him, in spite of what he had done, but her tongue was paralysed, her legs refusing to budge to make that vital movement which might distract the attackers and thus save Easton's life.

The door swung open further, caught by the wind, and she could see Valentine fighting, trying to thrust off the two in front of him, unaware of the third behind him until it was too late. Harriet saw him stiffen, swaying on his feet for a second like one drunk. Then he fell face downwards on the soggy earth, the dim light behind her just sufficient to ensure that she did not miss the final horror: a knife-handle sticking up from between his shoulder blades.

Harriet did not know how she got out of the chapel. Afterwards, when she thought about it, she had a vague recollection of the men moving in the opposite direction, thus giving her the chance of slipping out and running blindly through the churchyard again. She scarcely remembered mounting up, and all that she was conscious of during the ride back was the rude breath of the wind on her face.

She knew she could not go to the Hall, despite the fact that Michael Paris and the servants ought to be told what had happened. Someone else would have to do it; she could not face Valentine's house just then.

Instead, she left the horse at the gates and walked down

to Lantern House. She did not really like Bertha Drewhurst, for all her friendliness, but she had to go somewhere to recover from the dreadful sight and she could not bear Kate's loving concern just at that moment.

"My dear, how nice."

Bertha did not seem in the least surprised to see her, and when Harriet began a stumbled explanation, she waved it aside as she led the way into the parlour.

"I quite understand, and of course you were right to come here. I said that you should get out of that house, didn't I, and now you're here. Miss Batsby's here too, and Dr. Sawyer."

Harriet felt an explicable urge to run. She was not sure why, but there was something about the sight of Imogen Batsby and the doctor, sitting rigidly by the fire, which made her nerve-ends twitch. What were they doing there?

"Come and sit down," said Bertha, and nodded to her maid who was hovering in the background. "Some hot coffee for Miss March, Taylor. It's a cold night, and she's frozen through."

Harriet was grateful for the coffee, aware that although Bertha was rattling on with inanities, neither Sawyer nor Imogen had spoken since she had arrived.

She was just finishing the last of the coffee when Alfred Prewitt and Albert Melrose appeared. They looked somehow ruffled and less well groomed than usual, but the sight of their tousled hair did no more than remind Harriet of the still figure lying outside the chapel, and she put her cup down before her trembling hand could drop it.

When the two men were seated, there was a brief pause, and Harriet felt the dread inside her begin again. Why had

173

they all come? What were they doing at Lantern House at that hour of night? She was aware of something intangible in the air, very frightening and evil, yet they all looked so ordinary that she fought down her suspicions, forcing herself to believe it was the result of shock. It was because she had seen Valentine murdered; that was why she was so upset. It had nothing to do with the group round the fire who were staring at her with such fixity that she had to speak to stop herself from screaming.

"Perhaps I had better go, Mrs. Drewhurst. I was wrong to come here. I am disturbing you and your guests."

"Of course you are not." Bertha smiled knowingly. "They've come especially to see you."

"To . . . to see me?"

Harriet turned to look at the faces one by one. Imogen's was as petrified as her own; Sawyer's ruddy by the fire, eyes half-closed; Prewitt and Melrose watchful.

"I don't understand."

"Well, dear, I said I would arrange it, didn't I? And now we are all here, we can begin."

"Arrange what? Begin . . . I . . . don't know what you mean."

Harriet tried to get up, but it was as if she were fastened to the chair, and Bertha smiled again.

"The séance, of course. Have you forgotten? You asked Miss Batsby to try to find out where young Jonathan was."

"Yes, yes, but not now."

"Why not? We're all here. What better opportunity? Taylor, the lights."

"No!"

"There, there." Mrs. Drewhurst was soothing as the gas-

174

lights went out one by one. "I know you're upset about the boy, but don't you worry. I'm sure Miss Batsby can help. Come, everyone, let's sit round the table."

"I don't want to . . . not now."

Harriet managed to stand up, but someone took her arm and, instead of making for the door, she found herself sitting down, obediently stretching out her hands on the table to complete the circle.

She could not think why she was doing it, for although it was true that she had asked Miss Batsby for help, this was no moment to be participating in a séance; not with Valentine lying dead in the churchyard. Something uneasy touched her mind again. How had Mrs. Drewhurst known that she would come? Why were the others there? She forced the nagging worry away again. Probably Bertha hadn't had any idea that she was coming, and was simply entertaining friends, seizing the opportunity for the séance when she, Harriet, had unexpectedly arrived. And, after all, she had asked Imogen to try to reach Jonathan.

She sat very still, waiting for something to happen. She knew it must be very late now, nearing midnight. She was wondering why she thought time so important, when soft music began to play. This was nothing new, of course: she'd heard it before at Lantern House, but that night it seemed different. It was a quiet and awful lament, and she wanted to shout to Mrs. Drewhurst to make it stop, because it made her think again about Valentine, who had died without knowing that she loved him.

When the voice came, it was high-pitched like a child's, and Harriet stiffened.

"I'm Jonathan."

"Yes, dear." Mrs. Drewhurst was as bland as ever. "We hoped you would come. Where are you?"

"A long way away."

"Do you know where?"

"I'm not sure."

Harriet was shivering. One part of her mind recognised the fraud, but the other part refused to turn aside the chance of talking to Jonathan.

"Jonathan! Where are you?"

"Hush, hush." Mrs. Drewhurst cautioned her at once. "Be very quiet, or he'll go away. Yes, Jonathan?"

"I think I'm in. . . ."

The thin treble broke off abruptly as the candle went out, and Harriet called out again in desperation.

"Jonathan!"

"Be still." Mrs. Drewhurst was stern now. "Don't make a sound. I've told you many times how dangerous it is for Miss Batsby if you speak. No one must interrupt the voices of the dark."

Harriet was aware of the heavy breathing of Prewitt and Melrose on each side of her, feeling the total blackness wrapped round her like a shroud.

Then someone began to speak again, but this time it was not Jonathan's voice but that of a young girl.

"It's very cold here in the chapel."

Harriet heard Mrs. Drewhurst's involuntary gasp, but she herself was too stunned to move or even cry out.

"Why don't you let me go? You know who I am, don't you? I'm Daisy. I don't want to stay here with the dead. They won't speak to me, and it's so cold . . . cold . . . cold."

Imogen Batsby was sobbing hoarsely, and Bertha Drewhurst's breath was like a harsh rattle in her throat.

"I know what you're going to do with me." The girl's voice went on, regardless of the fact that no one had answered her. "You're going to send me to a whore-house in Belgium, aren't you, like you sent Ada and the others?"

Prewitt swore aloud, and Imogen's animal-like noises were growing louder. Harriet wanted to get up and run, but she had no strength left, not even enough to take her hands from the table.

Then she saw the light at the other end of the room, moving slowly towards her. The others were quiet now; even Imogen, as they all watched the dark shape coming nearer and nearer out of the gloom.

At that moment the light moved upwards, and they could see the contour of a face and the gleam of eyes picked up by the flame of the candle.

"No!"

Somehow, Harriet got to her feet, holding out a hand to ward off the apparition.

"No, no! You cannot be here, you can't be! It isn't possible. You're dead. Oh, dear God, you're dead, you're dead. . . ."

She had one last flash of consciousness, hearing Imogen Batsby's unearthly screams split the silence apart; then she fell headlong into a merciful oblivion where the appalling terror could no longer reach her.

The next day Harriet sat in the library at Easton Hall and looked up at Valentine. She still found it hard to accept that he was alive, but when he smiled at her in a way which he had never done before, part of the pain and disbelief began to fade as something warm and rather wonderful took its place.

"Did you sleep well?"

"Yes, I did. I don't remember anything about last night ...after...after...."

"No, you fainted. Michael brought you back to the Hall, and you roused long enough to drink some hot milk which he had doctored with brandy. We wanted to make sure that you slept, for you had had enough for one night. You've seen Jonathan?"

Her face lit up. "Oh, yes. He was asleep when I looked in just now, but yes, I've seen him."

"He's come to no harm. He's young and will get over it."

"But where was he? And you? I saw you die. Someone stabbed you with a knife and then...."

He held up his hand.

"I think I had better begin at the beginning. It is a long and not very pretty story. In fact, there are two stories really, neither very commendable."

He looked at her meditatively.

"Perhaps I should start with my part, to dispel some of the suspicions you have had of me."

She flushed. "I'm sorry if I...."

"Don't apologise. You had every right to doubt; every reason to suspect me." He gave a slight sigh. "Like all mysteries, it is very simple when one knows the answer. The man you saw last night was my brother Jason, Jonathan's father. We were very much alike, at least in appearance. Some time ago he was involved in a brawl in London. The other man was badly injured, and Jason thought he was going to die. Jason was hurt too, but he managed to get down here and demanded that I hid him until he was well enough to get a boat across to France. I didn't want to do it, but apart from the fact that he was my brother, he used Jonathan to force my hand. He threatened to tell the child what had happened if I didn't help him, and I did not think Jonathan could bear a burden like that."

Valentine's face had grown so cold that Harriet almost shrank back.

"You did not know Jason. Had you done so, you would have realised how violent and ruthless he could be. He was a man without scruples or reason. When he began to recover from his injuries, he insisted on going out. He said he was not an animal to be kept in a cage. I tried to stop him."

"But where was he?" Harriet could see the hurt in Valentine and wished she could touch his hand to reassure him. "Where was he hiding?"

"In the west turret."

"But it was empty. I saw that for myself."

Easton relaxed, the icy anger gone again.

"So you did, but you also saw another door, if you remember. I told you it was a store, but it wasn't. It led to other rooms, and that was where Jason was living. The voices you and Jonathan heard were Jason's and mine. We quarrelled when he insisted on leaving the house. I was afraid of what he would do. When the story of the lights began, I went to the chapel myself one night, for I thought it was Jason, but there was no sign that anyone had been there."

"Did he kill Eliza and Ada?"

"No, nor was he guilty of Margaret's death or Samuel Forest's, although Michael and I thought he was. We both knew what kind of man Jason was, and after he came down here he seemed wilder and less controlled than before. After a while, we thought he was growing mad. He no longer seemed interested in getting to France; it was as if he had some special reason for staying here, and we imagined it was connected with what was happening in the village. Michael urged me to give him up, and I had almost agreed, but then Jonathan disappeared and we thought his father had taken him. He was capable, even of that. In the end, we found he was blameless, and that's where we come to the second and even less palatable tale. Are you sure you want to hear about it?"

"Quite sure," she said firmly. "I am not always as feeble as I was last night. I had had a bad shock; I thought you were dead. . . ."

She broke off in some confusion, but he did not appear to have noticed that she had given herself away.

"Very well. The truth behind all that has happened is that Imogen Batsby, Alfred Prewitt and Albert Melrose were white-slave traffickers. You may not realise it, but trading in young women is a growing scandal, but it is a very profitable affair, and the authorities are not finding it easy to stamp it out."

"What!" Harriet sat upright. "You cannot be serious! Imogen?"

"Indeed I am. They had a small but lucrative business in London, using the séances as a cover. Imogen could have any number of strangers visiting her without creating the slightest suspicion. They would persuade young girls to take jobs abroad, as ladies' maids or something similar. The girls had to sign a paper indicating their consent, but when they crossed the Channel they found their employment was to be

180

something very different. Then a rival organisation forced them to leave London. Imogen had other reasons for going, which I will explain later. She was on her way to the coast when she came through Easton Mallet and it occurred to her that it was the ideal place to continue their work. Quiet, isolated, near to the Channel, with a disused chapel to keep the girls in overnight whilst they were waiting for the ship to dock."

"I saw a man in the village one day, talking to Prewitt and Melrose. Was he the captain of the ship?"

"Yes, he was. Unfortunately for Imogen, no sooner had she arrived than Mrs. Drewhurst recognised her. Bertha had seen the seamy side of life herself, and had lived in London before coming here. How she made her money we are not yet sure, but it is certain that it was not honestly. She promptly moved in on them, threatening exposure if they did not agree. Imogen hated her, but I think the two men respected her. She was shrewd, with a good head for business. It was her idea to get a hearse. It served two purposes: one to convey the girls to the chapel unseen, the other to ensure that the villagers kept to their homes at night."

"But if the girls were willing why did they have to be hidden?"

"Partly because Bertha was very cautious and partly because the girls sometimes changed their minds. Now and then one of them would realise what was going on, but by then it was too late to let her go, and so she was drugged and kept prisoner. Sawyer was an easy mark for them. Sometimes Prewitt and Melrose would meet the captain of the ship at the chapel; that is how it got its reputation for being haunted."

"But not by Fred Humble." Harriet gave a small laugh. "What about him?"

"A gift from the gods for Bertha and company. They made sure that the story of Fred was built up to terrify everyone around here, although Bertha always pretended to scoff at it. She preferred to blacken my name, and to hint that I was responsible for what happened to Eliza and the other girl."

"Oh, yes, Eliza. What did happen to Eliza and Ada?"

"They were taken abroad. That was Bertha's idea. Imogen and the others didn't want to take local girls, but Bertha was greedy. They were young and they were virgins. They would fetch a good price."

"What about Mr. Long?" Harriet was frowning. "How could so much go on in the chapel without him knowing?"

Easton shook his head. "That is perhaps the oddest thing of all, for if he'd been a different kind of man, Bertha and her friends would not have been able to do what they did. "I've spoken to him. The poor devil was scared out of his wits. He has confessed that he saw something one night and almost believed the story of Fred Humble. After that, he could never bring himself to go into the churchyard at night."

"Do you think Imogen really is a medium? Did she actually get in touch with the dead?"

"No. She is convinced that she has the gift, but it isn't true. Before every séance, Mrs. Drewhurst gave her a glass of wine. It was drugged, just enough to make her drowsy for fifteen minutes or so, whilst Bertha's groom crept into the rooms and produced the voices. He isn't a groom at all, of course, but an unsuccessful actor whom Bertha knew in

London. His one gift was mimicry. He could impersonate anyone, man, woman or child. It was useful to allay fears or create them."

"What about Rosie Forest and her father?"

"Rosie was out late one night, seeing her lover no doubt. We think she saw the hearse and it unhinged her mind."

"But before that? The man in her room? Were they after her, too?"

"They say not. I think that was Alastair Carrington. I had a letter from his uncle a few days ago. Carrington is still missing, and his uncle explained to me the kind of mental sickness from which he suffered. I don't think I should. . . ."

"Please, I'm not a child."

"He has an unnatural passion for young girls. Rosie probably attracted him."

"And Rosie's father?"

"Samuel was asking too many questions. Bertha and Prewitt were afraid that he might stumble on to something which could make him suspicious, and so they killed him. Sawyer knew what they had done, but he was too frightened of them to do anything but pronounce the death a mishap."

Harriet looked at Valentine uncertainly. She wasn't sure how to ask the next question, but he seemed to read her thoughts, for he said slowly:

"Margaret Lester's death wasn't an accident either. It seems that she had gone back to Lantern House after a séance to find her gloves. Later, Bertha found one of them outside her sitting-room and also realised that the door was ajar. She thought Margaret had heard her conversation with Prewitt and Melrose, so Prewitt got into Chase Lodge and

183

pushed Margaret downstairs. If the fall had not broken her neck, he would have done so."

"It is awful." Harriet meant it. She had not liked Margaret Lester, but she would not have wished that end for anyone. "I am so sorry that you. . . ."

"Be sorry for her, not for me," he replied briefly, clearly unwilling to pursue the subject. "Now what else is there to tell?"

"Jonathan, of course. What happened to him? Where was he?"

"In the chapel. Beyond the room you were in there was another store. They locked him in there. When Jonathan went out that night, he not only saw the hearse, he saw Prewitt driving it. Prewitt couldn't stop to catch him then, but he took him from the grounds soon afterwards, in case the boy plucked up enough nerve to tell us about it."

"Why didn't they kill him?" Harriet's voice was low, the very thought of it twisting her heart in pain. "Why did they keep him alive?"

"They were going to send him abroad. Young girls are not the only . . . well . . . they had a use for him."

"Oh, my God!"

"I told you it wasn't a pretty story."

"Yes, you did. What happened at the séance last night? Was it Mrs. Drewhurst's groom imitating that girl?"

"Indeed not. By then I had taken your advice and sent for the police. Things were getting out of hand and I knew I would have to turn Jason over to them. When we found him gone, we began to look for him and discovered his body at the chapel. We also found the captain of the ship and forced him to talk. The girl, Daisy, was not dead, only

184

drugged. When she recovered, she agreed to help us, and we brought her back to Lantern House to confront Bertha. When we realised that a séance was going on, we decided to give Bertha a taste of her own medicine. Daisy was a brave child, and although she'd had a bad time, she was willing to do her part."

"I was terrified." Harriet admitted it ruefully. "I knew it couldn't be Imogen, because I could hear her crying. I really thought for a moment it was a voice from the dead."

"Yes, I'm sorry we couldn't warn you, but there was no opportunity."

"How do you know so much about what happened?"

"Simple enough. What the captain and Sawyer did not tell us, Imogen did. She is a very frightened woman." He explained briefly the story of Mrs. Smith and her son. "The irony of it is that James Smith killed himself a week after his wife was hanged. One of the inspectors who came down here to-day remembered the case quite well. Imogen did not know that, of course. Her nerves were stretched to breaking point, and it has been a relief to her to confess everything, even down to the way in which the séances worked, with guitars and flowers coming through a trap door in the ceiling."

"Did Mrs. Lester know about Bertha and the others?"

"No, I doubt if she heard anything really, or if she did, she said nothing to anyone. No, it was me Margaret was blackmailing. She knew Jason was here. She must have seen him out riding one night, and she was aware what kind of man he was. She wanted me to marry her; that was the price of her silence. I refused. My *affaire* with her was over and I had no intention of making her my wife."

185

Harriet changed the subject quickly.

"Why did Mrs. Drewhurst want me to go and live with her? She seemed very insistent, and even offered me clothes which she said belonged to her niece."

"They were the clothes for the girls being sent to the brothels. As to why she wanted you, I'm afraid that was for the same reason as Ada and the others."

Harriet's mouth opened silently.

"You mean . . . I was to be sent to the Continent?"

"Yes. You are rather older than their normal victims, but you were too beautiful to pass over. They would have got a very good price for you." For a moment he looked savage. "At least we were able to stop that."

"Yes, and I think I owe you my life, Sir Valentine." Harriet wanted to say more, but was not sure how to do so. "I am grateful."

"It is nothing." He stood up. "I have to go out now! there are still things to be sorted out with the police. Michael has had to go back to London. Dine with me to-night, Miss March, and I will answer any further questions you may have. Meanwhile, why don't you go and say good-morning to Jonathan?"

At eight o'clock, Harriet made her way to the library and opened the door. Valentine turned from his contemplation of the fire to watch her cross the room, his eyes narrowing slightly.

The satin and lace gown was unmistakably Worth, and the diamonds at her throat and in her hair would have paid at least a prince's ransom, if not a king's. He could smell the subtle perfume as she drew nearer, recognising from long experience its costliness.

"Well, well," he said finally. "It seems that you too have been keeping secrets, Miss March."

She blushed. "It has been in my trunk since I arrived; the dress, I mean."

"Unusual garb for one of your station."

He was smiling, waiting for her to continue, and she took a deep breath as she began her explanation.

"I am not really a governess."

"No?"

"No, the truth is that Kate Plum was my aunt's maid. When my father died, I went to live with Aunt Laetitia, and Kate and I became good friends. She is a wonderful person, you know."

"Go on."

"We used to write to one another now and then. When I got her letter about Eliza, and could see how terribly unhappy she was, I knew I had to help her. I wanted to find out what happened to the girl. Then I saw your advertisement. I realised that if I came here as myself, no one would tell me anything, whereas they might be careless in the presence of a governess, for no one notices them."

"I did," said Valentine quietly. "I often thought you were far too bold and self-possessed for someone in your position, but I had so much else on my mind I did not stop to enquire why that should be."

Harriet gave a faint laugh.

"Oh, dear, and I thought myself so meek and submissive." Her smile faded and he saw the sudden sadness in her eyes. "In the end, I didn't help Kate, did I? Do you think they will ever find Eliza?"

187

"I doubt it." He was very gentle, but he could not lie to her. "They will make enquiries, of course, but there is not a lot of hope."

"Poor Kate."

He saw the suspicion of moisture on her lashes and changed the subject quickly.

"What can your aunt have been thinking about to let you embark upon such an escapade?"

Harriet forced herself to stop thinking of Kate and Eliza.

"She doesn't know I did, of course. I told her I was going to stay with friends in Scotland, and Aunt Laetitia is very old and absent-minded.

"The risk was frightful." He sounded almost angry. "So many things could have gone wrong."

"But they didn't." She was comforting. "And after all, I was under your roof."

"So you were." The frown vanished. "I rather think you may be hopelessly compromised, Miss March."

"Oh, surely not." She looked at him in alarm. "A governess?"

"But you are not a governess, are you?"

"No, but. . . . Oh, well, I shall be leaving here to-morrow, so perhaps no one will find out what I have done, and so my reputation may not be entirely lost."

"Jonathan will miss you."

He was studying her face, watching the emotion which clouded the amber eyes. Even in neat poverty she had been beautiful; now she was breathtaking.

"I shall miss him too."

"Then in that case, stay here."

"As a governess?"

Their eyes met again for a long moment before Valentine shook his head.

"I think not," he said softly, "for you weren't particularly successful in that role. Shall we go in to dinner, my dear Harriet, and discuss the possibility of some more permanent and satisfactory solution to the problem? Jonathan is not the only one who would miss you if you went. I rather think I might miss you too."